Dan Hawk Psychic Detective

Deborah Jones

First published in Great Britain in 2023 by Wealden Strand Publishers @wealdenstrand

Paper Edition: ISBN 978- 1-9161801-8-5

THANKS TO

Ben Shockley who asked me to write a book based upon his screenplay. This has been a fascinating journey, interpreting the story and taking it into the form of a book. I am looking forward to seeing the film! Trailers can be found on YouTube. Dan Hawk/Britflicks.

Adam Dawson for the cover artwork and Nikki Noyce for the cover photography

At The Drop of a Hat Productions and The Edge Folkestone

CONTENTS

PROLOGUE

They say that when you die, it is as if you are walking down a tunnel, and you see lights and hear voices calling you. Was it like that for Becky, Hawk wondered? Did she hear Errol and Mary urging her on? Her beloved grandparents, who had brought her up on that island – her happy place? The island he had heard so much about but never seen? He hoped so. He couldn't bear to think of nothingness, not for Becky. So much vibrance and joy, snuffed out in a moment. That was what really got to him, the squalor of where it happened, how it happened. Those scum.

He stood on the platform at Folkestone Central, duffel bag at his feet, watching a seagull pecking at a discarded chip. Rats with wings, he used to say, to tease Becky, but she loved the cries of the birds. That, and the crashing of the waves on the shingle, made her think of her island. Funny how everything was in the past tense now. That morning, he had said goodbye to the sunny flat which he and Becky had called home. He had given her herbs and spices and precious Scotch Bonnet plant to their neighbour on the ground floor, a jazz singer.

'I'll look after it for you,' she told him, enveloping him in a fierce hug. 'And keep in touch. Let me know when you're back down this way.' It was so hard to keep it together when people were kind. The gruffness of his Superintendent had, in many ways, been easier to bear. 'Take as long as you need,' he'd said, when Hawk had handed in his badge and keys, but the ticket in Hawk's pocket this afternoon was one way.

As the train pulled out, Hawk took out his book. Dr Syn, a lucky purchase from Marrins bookshop. Must be over a hundred years since Russell Thorndike wrote them, Hawk thought, but he still had the power to draw you into the eerie landscape of the Romney Marsh. A landscape that lent itself to writing. Perhaps he might take up writing again himself one of these days.

His thoughts were interrupted by a scruffy individual, standing in the aisle, rather too close for comfort, shouting into his mobile. 'Are you telling me that you got me all the way down here for nothing? What do you mean, there's no money for audition expenses? Well, you can stuff your part up your…' The man had a pale and pasty look, as though he had been indoors for a long time.

The man's words were lost as the train pulled out of Sandling, and into a tunnel. Giving the seats on either side of the aisle a spiteful shove as he went, the would-be actor moved up the train, before Hawk had the chance to remonstrate. 'Good,' Hawk thought. 'I'm really not in the mood.' He settled back and immersed himself in his book. It stopped him thinking about his next step. Unusually for a man whose career in the police force had been guided by instinct and a sixth sense, he really did not have a clue.

At Charing Cross, he moved along like an automaton with the crowd. A couple were having a fond reunion under the clock. He stopped momentarily, remembering his first date with Becky, and then, turning away from the entrance to the underground, walked down the grubby steps into Villiers Street and past Gordon's Wine Bar, the oldest in London, or so the owner had told him and Becky. That had been Becky's first introduction to Malmsey. Oh dear. He smiled. She had never been great at holding her drink. He wondered about popping in, for old time's sake, before heading to his sister's, on the edge of the Fens. A voice was urging him on, though, and the little framed photo inside his jacket pocket – was he imagining this or was it his mobile – gave a slight buzz. 'Becky?' he murmured. 'Keep going, Dan,' came the reply. 'You know the way from here.'

Daylight was beginning to fade. Along the Embankment the lights were coming on. A group of office workers chatted excitedly as they waited to board one of the floating restaurants. He walked past Waterloo Bridge and his steps led him to a large white building. Years before, it had been part of Shell. Then it had been converted into apartments. He and Becky had spent many happy nights there with their old friend

Sonya. She'd left the force and got a job in private security – high end stuff, corporate espionage and, as she said, never looked back. She of all people would understand and wouldn't ask prying questions. That was what he needed right now, he reflected, as his feet sank into the plush carpet and he greeted the concierge.

1 KILLINGS

In his studio to the west of Hythe, Thaddeus Moncrieff, resplendent in an old paint-splattered smock and a green bandana, was working late. Classical music blared out of his cassette player. He conducted it with his brush in between painting. It was the only way he could cope with his task. He surveyed the large papier mâché mask on the stand in front of him. Not his usual sort of commission. However, needs must. Heating bills were soaring. As if they weren't expensive enough already.

'Just a little heavier on the orange here, I think,' he murmured, his lips pinched with distaste. He angled his brush. The rain was hammering down. Sheep had taken shelter in the ruins of the church behind the studio. He liked them; they were company. As the evenings were beginning to draw in, fewer visitors were coming. The closure of the plant nursery next door hadn't helped. The story was told locally that along the road nearby, in the fourteenth century, certain 'sons of perdition' had murdered the local priest, on his way to say Mass. On a night such as this, he could imagine it happening.

The telephone rang in the small lobby to the side of the studio. Thaddeus went over to answer it. After a short pause, a voice intoned:

'I am he, I am thee.'

'And good evening to you too, young man.' Thaddeus was from the generation that introduced themselves when making or answering telephone calls. He guessed, although it was difficult to tell, that his caller was not. 'I wondered when you might call.' He fiddled with the switch on the lamp on the shelf beside him. The light flickered, went out, and after a moment came on again. There was nothing for it; he would have to get the electrician in to sort this place out. More expense.

'I'm just applying the finishing touches now. I'm very pleased with it, and I think you will be too. What's that you say? You want a painting of the mask? Well, that will be extra, of course.

How much? All right, I think that would cover it. And,' he added, 'I can leave both items outside the front door as we agreed. Just put the money through the letter-box.'
After a pause, he added, rather testily: 'No, I cannot recommend a sculptor. I would suggest you look up the Creative Foundation in the telephone directory. If you possess such a thing.'
The light flickered again. Thaddeus forced himself to concentrate. 'Look, I have no interest whatsoever in who you are.' This client, whoever he was, was beginning to irritate him. 'Although, I did just wonder, why the urgency? Halloween is still a few…Hello?'
The caller had hung up. Thaddeus shook his head and went back to his painting, the cassette player now cranked up to its highest setting. People were incredibly discourteous nowadays. After a while, he set his paintbrush and palette aside and locked the studio up. He walked across the road, in pitch blackness, to his house. He hadn't meant to work on so late. As he opened the door, he had the curious sensation that somebody was watching him.
'You're imagining things,' he chided himself. It did seem recently as if his mind was playing the odd trick, but he had been told that this was not uncommon and that he should do more crosswords or take up a foreign language. Neither appealed. He put the kettle on and, looking for something stronger to go with it as a nightcap, walked along the corridor into the study in search of the rather fine bottle of malt someone had given him for his birthday. He stopped dead. The small watercolour of Gratitude Farm, out on the Marsh, was gone from the wall on the other side of the woodstove; in its place a smaller painting by Brian Oxley of Romney Marsh sheep, sheltering under some trees. That had been on the other side of the stove. You could see where the watercolour had been. That wall needed a lick of paint now. He racked his brains. Maybe he had sent the Gratitude painting off for that exhibition in Rye after all, with the Fred Cuming's Camber series. Resolving to make some enquiries tomorrow, he went

back to the kitchen, malt in hand.

Some weeks later, Beverley Katharine Smithe, holding her little boy's hand tightly, was inside Peterborough Cathedral and making her usual beeline for the tomb of Katharine of Aragon. They'd come straight from nursery. It was dusk already; the nights were drawing in. She would stop and say a prayer today. She had a lot to be thankful for, after all.

Having been raised as a Roman Catholic, and because they shared names, Beverley felt an affinity with the Spanish queen. She had also been captivated by the story about the tomb having been vandalised by Cromwell's troops and then restored, a couple of hundred years later, after a fundraising campaign which had appealed to 'the Katharines of England' by one of the Cathedral Canon's wives. The Katharines of England – now that had a ring to it. Someone should write a play. Maybe she could write it herself.

'Look, Mummy, a pumpkin,' her little boy called.

'That's a pomegranate, darling,' she said absently. 'The symbol of Queen Katharine. Lots and lots of pips in a pomegranate.'

'It's a pumpkin,' he insisted. She looked up. Above the tomb, there was indeed a small stone carving of a pumpkin, tastefully done. She had never noticed it before although somehow it looked as if it belonged. Why on earth, though, would someone would have put it there? How strange. Deciding to dispense with the prayer this evening, she turned to her little boy.

'Come on. Let's go and get a hot chocolate.'

'Yay,' her little boy replied. As they turned to make their way towards the exit, Beverley paused. The choir, up by the main altar, was practising a hymn, Veni Creator Spiritus, one which Katharine would surely have recognised. Nearby, a figure in billowing black robes was sitting in a nearby pew. 'I am here to avenge an egregious wrong,' it droned. The last thing Beverley heard, as the figure loomed in front of her, was: 'I am he, I am thee.' She barely had time to scream, and the little boy was too frightened.

It was a few moments before the verger, who was getting ready for the evening service, came upon the grim scene. It reminded him in an awful way of the pietà he had seen in the summer at the Duomo in Florence. All the little boy could say was 'Pumpkin Man.' It was unfortunate that the security cameras were not working in that area of the Cathedral. The lady in the gift shop around the other side of the building later mentioned a man with a long, unkempt beard running past her.

A day later, and many miles to the south, John Carlton-Jones, reluctant teacher of Theatre Studies at the Westway Academy, was shepherding a group of Year 10s around the London Dungeon; more like herding cats than sheep. On school trips, no matter how interesting he tried to make them, the kids' main goal was to get through to the gift shop as fast as possible, to purchase or sometimes steal packets of lurid-coloured sweets. This morning's trip to the Globe had been no exception. This afternoon's Dungeon trip was meant to have been a reward for good behaviour. He would have curtailed the outing after lunch. The Deputy Head had vetoed his suggestion.

With any luck though, his teaching days were numbered. All being well, he would be giving his notice in at half term and say goodbye to this shower. For now, he had to get through this afternoon's special billing, a trial and an execution. Oh joy. They – and several other tourists - were to play the part of members of the audience. Unfortunately, his charges did not seem to be getting into character at all, already remarking that they were bored. Two of the girls also commented that they didn't like dungeons and that they felt sick. Nobody was taking any notice. The Deputy Head had linked up with a few American tourists and was bawling 'String him up,' her eyes shining with malice. That, John thought, spoke volumes about the woman.

With a sigh, he positioned himself to the side, near one of the exits. Somebody should at least be making some attempt at supervision. A couple of the boys, hovering at the edge of the group, had their mobiles out. They were meant to have left them on the coach and in any case in this part of the Dungeon, photography was forbidden. He opened his mouth to remonstrate. No words came.

'Sir?' James Cormack, although by no means a keen Theatre Studies student, was a kind boy and concerned to note that, over in the corner, Mr Carlton-Jones had slumped to the ground. It was so dark and noisy in there, nobody else had noticed. He put his phone back in his pocket and started pushing his way through the baying mob to get to him, but it was like trying to swim against a tide. He brushed past a figure in black flowing robes and an orange pumpkin mask. How odd. He was about to get his phone out and take a picture, but one of the teaching assistants, who had well and truly got into character, shouted in his ear. 'We paid good money for this spot, you idle wastrel. Get back over there now.' Resisting the temptation to scream at the daft old bat, James kept pushing. It was several moments before he reached his teacher.

Sidney Hester, landlord of the Shepherd's Hut, glanced at his watch. Just coming up for eleven. 'How time flies when you are enjoying yourself,' he thought. Set back off the road, on one of the only drovers' tracks on the Romney Marsh that had escaped being ploughed over in 1914, the Hut was a successful locals' pub. Other local landlords had, with varying degrees of success, gone down the 'gastro pub' route. However, at the Hut, part of the large kitchen had been converted into a bedroom and an en suite. In any case, Sid preferred to build his reputation on keeping a good cellar. A large jar of pickled eggs stood on the bar to satisfy the appetites of peckish punters. Packets of crisps and pork scratchings were always available. There had been favourable reviews on tripadvisor and on real ale websites. 'Excellent beer in a friendly, quirky pub.' He could live with a few quirks.

Sometimes, those with an interest in military history would look in for a pint. In 1941, a Messerschmitt had crashed nearby. Tales were still told of that night, kept alive by those far too young to remember, and how the pilot, who had survived the impact, had been rounded up by the locals and locked in the back room of the Hut until the Home Guard arrived. Soldiers, airmen and a few land girls stared out, forever young, from framed photographs which bedecked every wall.

On the wall behind the bar was a Falklands shield and pennant, and a grainy photograph of Port Stanley. Word was that this was how Sid had ended up in a wheelchair. 'Special forces,' some would suggest, as if they had inside knowledge, but Sid never enlightened anybody, preferring to keep his own counsel. Once, a local had introduced him to a visiting cousin, who had been in the Welsh Guards and on board the Sir Galahad. The pair had exchanged a few quiet words, in the way old soldiers do, and shaken hands. With the tenancy of the Shepherd's Hut, Sid had inherited a pot man, Fred Barnes, an old boy who cycled over every day, rain or shine from Burmarsh, and kept everything spick and span. Fred would also cover for him if he took the odd break. He only had to mention the phrase 'regimental reunion,' and Fred would be over at the double.

Tonight, only one table was occupied. Pete Wallace and Jackie, his missus, were in their usual spot by the door, with a chap Sid recognised but could not put a name to. 'How about a lock-in, Sid?' they called, but Sid shook his head. Not tonight. At the bar, Charlie Green finished his pint. He was swaying slightly. Before he could even think about ordering another, Sid wheeled himself out from behind the bar.

'You off then, Charlie?'

'Well, I did say I would be home half an hour ago,' Charlie replied. 'Got an audition tomorrow morning. Early start. You know the score.' He looked around him, as if trying to elicit admiration from an audience. None came. As he headed towards the door, Pete stopped him.

'Be careful out there, Charlie. Oooh.'

The others chuckled.

'You keep saying that, Pete.' He glared at Pete and his companions. He was tired of being the butt of their jokes. 'Why would anyone want to hurt me?'

'Well, you never know…'
Sid weighed in. 'Take no notice, Charlie.' Charlie and Pete were like oil and water. They'd all had enough to drink. Frankly, he had had enough of the lot of them. Perhaps he should call time now. Charlie stalked out, slamming the door behind him hard. The temperature in the bar seemed to have dropped several degrees, the jocular mood gone 'Pete, why do you always start on him?' Jackie began. 'It isn't even funny.'
Pete stood up.
'I'm going for a slash,' he announced. Jackie and their table companion got up and left while he was in there, coats buttoned against the chill.
'Night, Sid,' they chorused. Sid gave them a friendly wave. Jackie and Pete lived in a neat bungalow along the main road, the closest of the punters to the pub. Its lawns were mowed with precision and their hydrangeas always drew admiring comments in the summer. 'Cheerio, Pete, mind how you go,' Sid called, when Pete emerged, some moments later. He wheeled himself over to the door and bolted it behind his last customer.

The heavy rain of the previous weeks had given way to colder, crisper weather. Charlie was glad of his decent coat – purchased the other day, on the strength of tomorrow's audition. He had shot to fame some years before, in a children's television series, set in an isolated Welsh valley. Slightly 'retro,' it had aired on Sundays in the teatime slot and captured the imagination of the public. It had paid enough for him to buy a house, mortgage-free, in this quiet corner of Kent, but recently work had dried up. However, he had it on the qt from the director, an old friend from way back, that tomorrow would be less of an audition and more of a shoe-in. The play – Slaybrook – was an imagined episode in the life of Noel Coward at the time when he wrote Blithe Spirit. The director had explained that he wanted a complete mix of experienced and new actors. 'I'm counting on you as a steadying hand, Charlie boy,' he'd added.

'Steadying hand,' he'd chuckled. 'Moi?'
Charlie tried to remember a few lines from Blithe Spirit as he staggered along. There was a line about 'mystic ships.' Appropriate for the countryside around here; it had all been under water once, hadn't it? His house, which had been converted from two cottages, was solid enough and square, like something a child would draw. Down the track and over a stile, as if that would sober him up. The walk back from the Hut always made him think of a poem he had learnt at school about the rolling English drunkard and the rolling English road. He tried to remember the lines and was about to declaim them – good practice for tomorrow – when he became aware of somebody walking behind him. He quickened his pace. The person behind him quickened their pace too. Thinking it might have been Pete messing about, he turned. He spotted a figure in a long, flowing cape, with what appeared to be a pumpkin for a head.
'I am he, I am thee,' the figure intoned.
'Jesus Christ!' Charlie began to run. It wasn't far now to the house and he was in reasonable shape. He looked over his shoulder. There was no sign of his pursuer. 'Phew,' he breathed. 'Outran him.' He shook his head and slowed to a walk. Moments later, he opened his mouth to scream as the figure reared up in front of him, brandishing a razor. He fell to the ground, his throat slashed. The figure bent over him, appearing to write something on his forehead, and then vanished.

2 HOMECOMING

As the train pulled into Folkestone Central, Hawk's attention was caught by a colourful sign, clearly meant to attract the young, the hip and the creative. It was unfortunate that somebody had defaced it, so that it read: 'Folkestone is a Shart School.' Alighting onto the platform, duffel bag slung over his shoulder, he smiled. Nothing much had changed then, by the sounds of it, in the intervening years.

Turning up at Sonya's London flat those few years ago had been fortuitous; she'd been about to leave for Geneva to set up and run a branch office for the investigation agency she worked for. Money no object, by the sounds of things. 'You'd be doing me a favour,' she told him. 'Saves me having to get a tenant. I know you'll look after the place.' And so, Hawk had stayed. A modest inheritance from his Mum, who died not long after Becky, had kept him going, and then there was the writing.

Some years before, he had sat with Becky and Sonya in the café at the Tate Modern, drinks in hand, looking down at the tiny figures below and the old house on the other side of the river. They all speculated as to who had lived in it over the years. Important, wealthy men in Puritan collars and then in tailcoats as the centuries rolled on, but Hawk had a strong image of a servant girl, in a dove-coloured dress who had been accused of stealing an emerald necklace. Sonya and Becky listened, entranced. 'I can almost reach out and touch her, the way you describe her,' Becky commented. 'You should write this down.' Hawk did just that. After some of the shifts at the police station, writing came as a relief. He wrote Molly Benson's story in the style of one of those chapbooks they used to sell outside Newgate prison at an execution.

A friend of Sonya's had helped Hawk put his novella onto amazon and had put it in for the South Kent Scribblers' annual award. It won, much to his surprise, and earned him his first meeting with literary agent Victor Barkley, in a ramshackle office near Leicester Square. Vic's reputation for talking nineteen to the dozen, especially when he was enthusiastic about a new writer, preceded him. That first meeting was no exception. Many ex-coppers had a yearning to write, he often said, but their prose could be leaden and pedestrian. Hawk's talent shone out.

'You write with your heart and soul, young man. Now, Molly Benson was impressive -very Hilary Mantel - but historical novels are a bit niche. Women tend to read them, and it's a funny thing, but they often prefer books written by women. You need to settle on a genre. Misery memoirs have been and gone,' Vic continued, 'and so have those 'girl about town' books. Why not write what you know? Police novels seem to be catching on again. Bit of grit to liven things up. How about it?'

Hawk had promised to think about it, but, as happens to so many writers, life got in the way. At work, his star was in the ascendant, with promotion in the offing. Like many police officers, Hawk had 'hunches.' His, however, were uncannily correct. It was as if he could see into people's minds, with the scene of the crime unfolding like a film in his head. He tried not to take work home with him, but sometimes he had the most vivid of dreams. The time had come though when he hadn't acted on his hunch. That was when the darkness had descended. It had stayed ever since.

A few months after Becky's death, Hawk called in at Gordon's Wine Bar one evening, on an impulse. It was on a circuit he did every day from Sonya's flat, along the Embankment. It was there that he had a chance encounter with Vic. 'Come on,' Vic urged. 'How about that cop book? Come and see me at the office.' He was having none of Hawk's protestations. 'Monday morning at ten,' he said, as they parted. 'Be there.' As he walked home, Hawk felt the tiniest buzzing from the photo he kept in his pocket and he heard Becky's voice. 'Forward, not back, Daniel Hawk. Make it fun. You can do it.'

And so, Mr Pumpkin Head was born, starting with The

Pumpkin of the Marsh, in a nod to Russell Thorndike. Something of a vigilante, Hawk's creation was rather a menacing figure in a flowing black cape, with a pumpkin for a head, who terrorised the Romney Marsh and the rest of the Kent coast, the Fenlands, certain stretches of the Thames and other 'liminal places' (Vic's phrase but the young editor at the new and up and coming publishing house lapped it up.) Deals were signed, and the money began to flow in. Hawk never ceased to be amazed at the popularity of his creation, and its constant ability to outwit the local constabularies. Mr Pumpkin Head's fame was spreading overseas, and Hawk had recently returned from another tour in Spain. On an impulse, and with Brexit on the horizon, he had purchased a small 'pied à terre' in Girona. He'd felt that slight buzz again from Becky's photo. 'Great idea, Dan,' she'd told him. 'Just make sure you wear your cap in the sun.'

This time last week, fortified by tapas and a large glass of tinto, Hawk had climbed the ninety steps up to the cathedral, wearing the cap Becky had bought him a few years back, wondering whether and how Mr Pumpkin Head might make an appearance on the Iberian Peninsula. Perhaps he could appear in a Mardi Gras parade, or in a Day of the Dead procession, although wasn't that more of a Mexican thing and might it offend sensibilities? Was Halloween a big thing over there? Would that really matter?

Still pondering, Hawk had flown back to London and then on to Peterborough for a book-signing. The fourth and most recent book, Rousing Hereward, had been set in the Fens and in the town itself, with a dramatic scene outside the Cathedral, the last resting-place of Katharine of Aragon. The significance was not lost on him, funny how so many themes and events in his life were linked. One of Mr Pumpkin Head's victims in this area had been an archaeologist turned grave robber, who had a theory, that became an obsession, that Katharine had not been buried alone. Mr Pumpkin Head had also come face to face in Rousing Hereward with a giant Green Man, who had been making his way across the country into East Anglia. The book had ended on a cliff-hanger, with the suggestion of a reappearance in the next book for Mr Pumpkin Head in his more familiar territory of the Romney Marsh. Hawk had planned a few walks in the area for research. He would have to steel himself – he and Becky often used to cycle out that way.

Now, after another signing in London, he was back on his old patch. Today's signing had been arranged in Folkestone, at Marrins Bookshop. It seemed fitting somehow – after all, an early scene in the first book took place on Folkestone's Warren, on a dark and stormy night when some wild campers had come across a figure in a black flowing cape, standing on the concrete apron, staring out to sea. Hawk's steps slowed as he approached the shop. He had spent many a happy hour in there. Becky had loved it too. He tried the door; it was locked. They'd said eleven; he was a couple of hours early.

He made his way along Sandgate Road and down the Old High Street towards the Harbour, noticing a busy coffee shop on his right. Writers were already gathering there with laptops and notebooks. Perhaps he would pay a visit after the signing. The cakes looked delicious. Down on level ground, he looked around and took stock. The Harbour Inn had been done up. Chummies was still there. He closed his eyes for a moment, remembering his nan, whose 'not so secret' pleasure had been a portion of jellied eels and whelks from the stall, which had been somewhat less elaborate in those days.

Breathing in the salty air, he walked on, at a pace. He paused in his perambulations at the Leas Lift – what a shame the gates were still closed. He remembered the fund-raising beer festival he had been to there with Becky, a few years before. The place had been drunk dry within a few hours, and he smiled at the memory of the group of friends they'd been with. They'd had to dissuade one girl, drunk on happiness and Kentish cider, from stripping off and going for a skinny dip. A brisk walk back up the Road of Remembrance took Hawk onto the Leas. Work had started on the Leas Pavilion Theatre, with the compromise of flats being built on top. He stopped for a moment and looked at the billboard, wondering how this was

going to work. There were so many new developments going up now. 'If they keep building like this,' he thought, 'I'll struggle to recognise the place.'
He stood for a moment by the memorial arch and glanced at his watch. Enough time for a coffee and a bacon sarnie before going back to Marrins. He noticed a café where people were sitting outside in the sun. He went inside, put his order in and sat down at a table in the corner. The waitress brought his order over and, as he ate, he glanced at a newspaper someone had left behind. He almost spilt his coffee. 'Mr Pumpkin Head strikes again,' the headline announced. The article reported killings in Peterborough, London and Folkestone over the past few days. The victims had been found with their throats cut. The reports of the Peterborough and London cases mentioned a person in black in the vicinity, wearing a pumpkin head mask. Someone had spotted the link. There was a picture – obviously scanned in in quite a hurry – of The Black Heart of Blackfriars, his second book.
'For fuck's sake,' Hawk exclaimed, as he went to pay for his breakfast. 'Do excuse me, ladies,' he apologised, to a group which may have been from the local Women's Institute and which was tut-tutting at his language. Writers, Vic Barkley had told him over a pint or two, often think of their creations as puppets and themselves as puppet-masters. And here was Mr Pumpkin Head, cut loose from his control and on the rampage. What a nightmare. He turned his steps towards Marrins. This time, the door was open, and his old mucker Bill was waiting for him. Bill clapped him on the shoulder.
'It's so good to see you again,' he exclaimed, leading Hawk over to a small table in the window. 'We've missed you here. Now, I've got a few pens for you; they always go walkabout on these occasions. I'm expecting trade to be steady today – this has been well-advertised. And you're a celebrity now. Can I get you a cuppa?'

Half a mile down the road from the Shepherd's Hut, the forensics team had been hard at work. Detective Constable

Jennifer Reeves had parked up on the other side of the taped-off area. The Family Liaison lot were still with the victim's wife and they'd already spoken to the publican and the punters who had been in the Hut the night before. Relatively new to the Folkestone police force, following a transfer from the Met for 'personal reasons' and still trying to find her feet, DC Reeves was relieved this morning to find herself paired up with Detective Sergeant Sam O'Neal. In the six years he had been in Folkestone, DS O'Neal had worked diligently and risen steadily through the ranks. He had also grown to know the area like the back of his hand. Some said that he lacked imagination, but in their line of work, hard facts were what counted, and O'Neal was certainly methodical.

With her petite frame and a gamine haircut, DC Reeves could pass in the right light for twenty-five. Actually, she was getting on for forty. She watched DS O'Neal walking towards her. Oh no. With him was Kyle Petrie, a young colleague, young being the operative word. Awkward or what? They'd been on a couple of dates which had led nowhere. Kyle stooped down and leaned into the window. They exchanged a few desultory words, before O'Neal unwittingly rescued her by getting into the passenger seat. Kyle took the hint and wandered off. Reeves took a deep breath.

'What's the score then, sir?'

O'Neal explained that they were still collecting samples. The victim's throat had been cut, and, as with the London and Peterborough killings, the word NEXT! was written on his forehead. No fingerprints had been found at the scene. This time though, there were no witnesses, not even a fleeting glimpse of anything out of the ordinary.

'So,' mused Reeves. 'Mr Pumpkin Head strikes again, by the looks of things. It's almost as if he is a ghost.'

O'Neal seemed distracted. 'Bloody newspapers, where do they get their information from? They can never be arsed to check it properly. Folkestone's a long way from the Marsh, you'd have thought they'd have known that…anyway, I'm really not sure how we'll tackle this.'

'Speaking of ghosts,' Reeves began, 'it was before my time, but do you remember a cop who used to work down here by the name of Dan Hawk?'

'Dan? Yes, I do remember him. He was into that psychic crap. Just went off the radar, disappeared. Shame really, I liked him.'

'Well,' she continued. 'He became an author and wrote those books about Mr Pumpkin Head.' She showed him the article in her newspaper. 'He's in Folkestone this morning, doing a book signing at Marrins.'

'Obviously meant to be then,' O'Neal commented. 'We might have a few questions for him. Best get going before he's finished there.'

He chucked the paper onto the back seat and Reeves drove off, along the winding Marsh lanes towards West Hythe. There was something timeless about it. They drove past an almost derelict house and a field full of sheep, stolidly munching grass. Soon they were on the A259. Reeves drove along Prince's Parade, a stretch of road she loved. A group had assembled for a sea swim. Apparently, the sea was still warm. Rather them than her. As they passed through Sandgate, she paused to let the number 16 bus go past and the driver gave her a friendly wave. Drivers were courteous down here, she liked that. Moments later, they were parking up outside Marrins. The bell rang as the shop door opened.

'There you are,' Bill nudged Dan. 'Even got the local constabulary interested.'

'Well, well, well,' O'Neal observed, as he approached the table. 'If it isn't Dan Hawk Psychic Detective.'

'Oh yes, DC O'Neal, isn't it? To what do I owe the pleasure? Come to buy a book?'

'DS O'Neal,' O'Neal corrected him, 'and this is DC Reeves. Long time no see. We need a chat with you. Might I ask, where were you yesterday and last night?'

'In London,' Dan replied. 'Came down early this morning.'

'And what about the day and night before?' asked Reeves.

'Look, what is this?' Hawk stood up. These two were beginning to get on his nerves.

'Just answer the questions.' O'Neal was clearly getting riled too. Hawk sighed.

'I was in Peterborough,' he told them. 'Doing a book signing, same as in London and here.'

With a flourish, Reeves produced her tablet and the headline 'Mr Pumpkin Head strikes again' flashed up. She pointed to the sub-heading, 'Killings in Peterborough, London and Folkestone' and shot Hawk an enquiring look.

'If I was the killer,' Hawk commented, 'it would be a bit stupid of me to kill people in the same town where I was doing my book signings. Wouldn't it?'

'He has a point,' Bill chimed in. Hawk broke the uncomfortable silence that followed. 'Look, let's go somewhere else and talk.'

'Good idea.' O'Neal turned to Reeves. 'Give me half an hour or so, just got a few things to run past Briggs.'

Reeves nodded. 'We'll go to Chambers. Nice tea in there.' She turned to Hawk. 'If you like tea, that is?'

'Fine by me.'

3 RECRUITED

Superintendent Briggs stood up, trying hard not to wince. His back really was killing him these days, but the last thing he wanted was anyone commenting on it.

'Absolutely,' he paused to give his words their full effect 'no way. Whatever has got into you, DS O'Neal? Not like you to go off piste.'

His words stung, but O'Neal ignored them and pressed on. 'At least could you just think about it, sir? Hawk's in town, promoting his latest book. I hadn't been here long when he left, but everyone here has always spoken highly of him. I know people used to joke about all the psychic crap…'Briggs raised an eyebrow. 'But I remember Detectives Tyronne and Edge particularly had a lot of time for him. And Detective Sellers too.'

Briggs moved towards the window and stared out of it. Two motorists were having an altercation in the street down below, oblivious to the traffic around them. From this height, they looked like angry Lego figures. Eventually, they both got back into their cars and drove off, waving tiny fists. 'We all had a lot of time for Hawk,' he said at last. 'So, what are you suggesting? A temporary reinstatement to help solve this case?'

'Yes, sir.' O'Neal swallowed hard, wondering whether he had overstepped the mark.

'It's most irregular. I don't think I've ever heard of anyone being temporarily reinstated.' Briggs fiddled with the cord on the blind; bloody thing was constantly jamming. 'Then again, how often does an ex-copper write books where his creation comes to life and starts killing people?' He swung round. 'And you're quite sure it isn't Hawk doing this?'

'Absolutely sure, sir. I've checked with Peterborough and the Met. He was at the book signings at the time of each murder. And last night he was in London at another signing.'

'I'll need to make some calls,' said Briggs, 'and run this up the line. I can't promise anything, mind. But in the circumstances, he might just be our best asset.'

In Chambers' basement, Hawk and Reeves sat together at a small table with their tea. Always busy with musicians in the evenings, during the day its nooks and crannies were ideal for a confidential conversation, away from prying ears. A busker Hawk vaguely remembered was perched on a stool at the bar. The man raised a hand in a half salute and went back to his conversation with the girl behind the bar.

'I've always wanted to know,' Reeves was almost beside herself, 'in The Black Heart of Blackfriars, why you chose…'

O'Neal sat down at the table. 'Sorry to interrupt,' he said, as a mug of tea was placed in front of him, so strong you could almost stand your spoon up in it. He sipped at it; it went down a treat after his contretemps with Briggs 'Just recapitulating then, somebody seems to have been following you around the country to your book signings.'

'And killing somebody in each town, hoping to pin the deaths on me.' Hawk finished his sentence for him.

'Whilst dressed up as your creation,' Reeves chimed in.

'Mr Pumpkin Head,' all three chorused.

'How are the victims killed?' Hawk asked.

'Just like in your books – and by the way I'm a massive fan of all of them – their throats are cut and there are no finger prints.' Reeves paused. 'The difference though is that the killer has been writing NEXT! on the victims' foreheads. Presumably he doesn't mean the shop.'

'We don't know that yet,' O'Neal observed, 'and with this latest killing on the Marsh, there are no witnesses. By the way, I've spoken to Briggs and to the Met and Peterborough. They will send us over what they have so far. They're happy for us to take it from here.'

'Us?' Hawk queried. He was genuinely puzzled. Barely half an hour ago, this pair had burst in on his book signing, implying some sort of involvement in the killings on his part. Now, they seemed to be including him in the investigatory process. 'You do know,' he continued, 'that my police badge and gun licence

were revoked?'
'Quite honestly, we're buckling under the pressure of lots of other cases down here.' O'Neal put his mug down and gave Hawk one of his level stares, 'and perhaps as you wrote the books the killer seems to be basing himself on…'
'I could help solve it.' Hawk reflected that he was making a habit of finishing people's sentences. Some might find that irritating. As for helping to solve the cases, Sonya had been on at him again to join her at the investigation agency. Perhaps he could go one better and set up on his own. Dan Hawk Psychic Detective, as O'Neal had styled him earlier, did have a certain ring to it. This could be his first commission. His head was spinning. 'I'll have to run this past my wife first.'
O'Neal and Reeves exchanged glances. 'Any help you need, here's my card,' O'Neal offered.
'Thank you, but I usually prefer to work alone.'
O'Neal looked over at Reeves. 'Well, we- that is Superintendent Briggs and I – were thinking more along the lines of putting DC Reeves here with you, as a sort of babysitter. And,' he turned to Hawk 'if you agree, the recommendation is that you are reinstated. On a one-off basis.'

Superintendent Briggs; still there then. And down here, they clearly still 'did things differently.' A one-off reinstatement; that was a new one on him. In for a penny, in for a pound, Hawk resolved. 'I'll get my badge back then?'
O'Neal nodded.
'And a gun?'
'Not a snowball's chance in hell,' O'Neal replied. 'You of all people should know the rules on that. Anyway, Reeves here is an AFO, as am I, so you need have no worries on the security front.'
Hawk opened his mouth to remonstrate but O'Neal hurried on. 'Look, Reeves will bring you your badge and we can probably sort some wheels out for you too. Just do whatever you can to help us bring this psycho bang to rights.'
After a very quick trip to the police station, to have his photo

taken and to sign a few forms, Hawk made his way to the B &B, on the East Cliff. He and Becky had lived in Bouverie Road West, more in the centre of things. This place was sufficiently removed from any associations although he remembered Pippa, the landlady, from the old days. Always short of space, he and Becky sometimes used to put visiting family and friends up here. Presumably, like just about everyone else, Pippa knew what had happened but as she led the way upstairs, she tactfully didn't mention it. She simply told him that his room had a nice sea view and that breakfast was at nine o'clock sharp. 'Full English or continental, just let me know a bit later. Not got anyone else booked in for the next couple of weeks, so you'll have the run of the place.'

He breathed a sigh of relief after she left him to unpack. Not that he had much with him, but he propped the little framed photo of Becky against the bedside light.

'I will be careful, I promise,' he told her. 'And yes, just this one case. I can't help feeling responsible.'

'I understand,' Becky replied. 'I'll try and help when I can. Oops, the signal is going a bit.'

'Becky?'

'I don't blame you for what happened to me…'

There was a crackling noise and her voice faded. Hawk sighed. He kicked his shoes off, lay down on the bed and closed his eyes.

'But I do blame myself, Becky. And I always will.'

He thought back to early November 2016. Bonfire Night had come and gone. A little too early for Christmas decorations – he remembered how Becky had loved them. An election coming up in the States, Britain arguing with itself over Brexit. Weather-wise, much like today – grey and depressing, with what the locals called a mizzle. He'd been in and out of meetings with Superintendent Briggs all day. A pub landlady had been murdered, up here on the East Cliff. A tightknit community up there, and if anybody did know anything, they weren't telling. 'We've got to come up with something and fast,' 'Super' Briggs had told him. He'd stayed on after his shift, going through the profiles O'Neal had been putting together but nothing had jumped out at him. He'd wandered up to the Unicorn, but apart from an old boy with no teeth playing a piano that was so out of tune it made him wince, and a bone-thin (and extremely deaf) barman in an old tweed suit that had seen better days, there was nothing doing.

Then he'd headed to the British Lion, to talk to Colin, his old mate at the Folkestone Herald, to see what he knew about the Unicorn and its landlady, a newcomer to the area. It seemed that ever since Victorian times, when a dwarf who went by the name of Popgun Billy had ruled the roost, the Unicorn had been a lawless place. Goods of various descriptions, and sometimes firearms too, were exchanged there and as the Kipling poem went, them as asked no questions weren't told no lies. In the Great War, word was that the community had sheltered the landlord's son whose mind had gone on the Western Front and who would not – could not – go back there. Before the EU and the abolition of duty free put an end to the necessity, Drunken Duncan, professional smuggler extraordinaire, could always be found at the Unicorn and could sell you as much tobacco as your heart desired.

Too far from the gentrification already under way on Tontine Street and around the Harbour, the Unicorn had continued to ply its trade. It had ticked over but the recession and the austerity that followed had meant that its clientele, no matter how loyal, struggled to keep it going. Then, the brewery had made a new appointment, in the shape of Isobel Entwhistle. Nobody knew very much about her, save that she was in her fifties, as tough as old boots and originally from Belfast. Her reputation, as somebody who could turn a place around and transform it from an old man's pub into a trendy destination bar, had preceded her. She had been doing precisely that in West London for many years. There were those who were unhappy with the plans, Colin told Hawk, but frankly, were any of them capable of murder?

'Perhaps they weren't,' Hawk suggested. 'Local, I mean.

Sometimes, people bring their problems with them.' The atmosphere in the British Lion had altered then; if there was such a thing as a pub barometer, its reading would have swung from 'convivial' to 'glacial.' Had his psychic powers kicked in then, he wondered afterwards, or had somebody had been earwigging? Colin had put another pint down in front of him. That had given way to another and another, and another, leading to a shocking hangover the next day.

He'd been woken up (what the hell was the time anyway?) by Becky moving around the flat, gathering her files and briefcase. Gingerly opening one eye, he'd asked:

'Where are you off to?'

'Meeting with Avelyn. I did mention it. I hope I don't get stuck there all day, like last time.'

'Good luck with that,' he'd murmured before sinking back into slumber. If only he had known that was going to be their last conversation; the banality of it upset him sometimes when, as he was still wont to do, he went over and over things in his mind.

Becky had a burgeoning business as a garden designer. The High-Speed link from St Pancras was beginning to attract people to come and live in the area. For many of them, it was the first time they'd ever had a garden. Avelyn Walter, Becky's client, was one of them. She had a PR agency (Becky had never been quite sure what was being promoted) and a small office in Tontine Street. She had recently bought a large house in Turketel Road from an elderly couple. Over the years, they had become overwhelmed by the garden and, rather than letting it become completely overgrown, they had turned it into something easy to maintain, with just one long flower border with a beautiful yellow standard rose. A blank canvas for Becky, although it had to be said that Avelyn was a demanding client. They'd had arguments over the rose, which Avelyn had wanted gone. Becky had persuaded her that with care it could be coaxed back to its former glory and they could make a feature of it. Hawk had suggested a few times that Becky should tell her where to go, but Becky, ever the consummate professional, had wanted to see the challenging assignment through. If only she'd listened to him.

Now, he looked over at her photo again and closed his eyes for a moment. Here he was, back on his old patch, about to be reinstated, at least for now, with Mr Pumpkin Head unchained and the book tour on hold. Time for the courtesy call he had been putting off for a while. He picked up the phone and dialled Vic Barkley's number.

'Great to hear from you, Dan. How's tricks? How was Girona? Had your fill of tapas and rioja? Still waiting for my postcard, you miserable toe rag.' Vic was in jocular mood. At least somebody was, thought Hawk. 'How's your book tour? What about all those grisly murders? As long as they keep pushing the sales up, eh?'

Hawk explained about the temporary postponement of the tour and how he'd be staying put in Folkestone for a while, to work on the case. 'It might just save some innocent lives,' he added. Vic suggested this could form the basis of the next Mr Pumpkin Head novel. Met with a stony silence, Vic quickly changed the subject to the movie rights and the speculation as to who might play Mr Pumpkin Head.

'I'd rather hoped it might be someone local,' Hawk replied. 'Ken Colley, Jessica Hynes perhaps, George Irving, Ben what's his name…otherwise…I don't know…Mark Benton, Bill Fellows or Miriam Margolyes? Maybe Robert de Niro?'

'Wrong on all counts.' Vic could scarcely contain himself. 'Are you seriously not following all the hype? Don't know who leaked the story the other day, but they've only bloody got Gavin Lloyd Goldstein!'

'You're fucking kidding.' Only the other day, Hawk had read an article about an intoxicated Goldstein staggering out of a London nightclub, a girl on each arm. One of them was named as Cindy Sinden, no relation to the distinguished actor, the article had said, but 'a model with the looks of an angel but the gob of a fishwife.' Goldstein had thrown some wild, badly-aimed punches at the photographers before toppling over and being dragged hastily into a taxi by the two girls. The headline,

which had caught Hawk's eye at the time, read; 'I love you, you b……. s, says Goldstein to decked paps.'
Vic pressed on. 'It's great, isn't it? Gavin says this is the role he was born to play.'
'No, Vic, it isn't great at all.' Like all authors, Hawk was protective of his creation, no matter how monstrous. 'The man's a liability. He drinks like a fish and, as he has famously said of himself, fucks like a stoat. Why can't they just cast someone local to here, where most of the books are set? And even if they couldn't, I mean, really…'
'Always the way, love.' Vic shrugged. Authors got so precious about things. Why they couldn't just go with the flow, he could never understand. After all, how many of them ever got into print, let alone on screen? A little appreciation wouldn't go amiss sometimes. 'Must dash. Keep you posted. And drop by the office soon, it's been far too long. Ciao, ciao!'
Downstairs, the doorbell rang, one of those you couldn't ignore; loud, insistent and bloody annoying. Clearly, Pippa never wanted to miss a thing. He could hear muffled voices downstairs.
'Dan,' she called. 'There's somebody to see you. A Detective Constable Reeves?'
'Delivery,' announced DC Reeves. His badge.
'Cheers, that was quick.'
'More bureaucracy, I'm afraid,' Reeves handed over yet another form for him to complete and sign and they went through into the kitchen in search of a pen and a clean surface.
'All sorted. Need a lift anywhere?'
'Well, I need to go out to the Marsh, to the murder scene, but until I can get a car sorted…'
'I'll drop you over there,' Reeves offered.
'Ah, I see. Babysitting.'
'We're not all dicks down here,' Reeves told him.
Pippa came through, looking apologetic. 'Something's come up. Family emergency. As you're going to be here for a few days, Dan, would you mind keeping an eye on the cat?'
'No problem.'

'That's great. I am sorry about this. I'll show you where everything is later. Cat food, breakfast things. By the way,' she continued, giving Hawk a wink. 'I'm pretty relaxed about overnight guests.'
Reeves cleared her throat. Awkward again - the story of her life. 'Super Briggs' had taken the opportunity earlier of filling her in on Hawk. 'There you have it,' he'd said. 'Two murders in close succession – and the second one was his wife.' Poor guy. It would be very difficult to get over something like that. It wasn't all that long since she'd extricated herself from a marriage she would now rather forget and then, a matter of weeks later, lost her Mum. She still found that hard. She cleared her throat and looked down at Pippa's terracotta floor tiles.
'I'll bring the car round,' she said, after a while.
'I'll get my coat,' Hawk replied.
'Why? You haven't pulled,' Reeves retorted, quick as a flash. Another silence. Not again. She cursed her clumsiness and hurried outside to wait for Hawk. Half an hour later, they were standing in the road. The tape and the crime scene tent had been cleared away, although a faint chalk outline of Charlie could still be discerned.
'This is where…' she began, rather unnecessarily, but Hawk wasn't listening. He took a deep breath. Next, he dropped to one knee. Each to their own, Reeves thought. 'Have you lost something?' she enquired, but Hawk was already straightening up. 'Only my sense of humour,' he replied. He walked off at a pace, leaving her trailing in his wake.
'Now where are you off to?' she called, as she followed him down the road, onto the drovers' track and into the Shepherd's Hut, where Sid was polishing glasses with precision. 'I'm afraid we're not open yet,' he called. Reeves and Hawk appeared in front of him and flashed their badges.
'We're just making some routine enquiries,' Hawk explained.
'Ah, this is about poor Charlie. Awful business. Who on earth would have meant him any harm, a nice man like that?' He set the glass he had been polishing down neatly on a brass tray and

added: 'He was in here just before he died.'
'I sensed he was,' Hawk replied. Sid gave him a strange look, but Hawk did not elaborate. After a moment, Sid wheeled himself to the other end of the bar to fiddle with one of the optics.
'Wait a minute, I know you,' Sid turned around. 'You're that psychic writer. Dan Hawk. You write those Pumpkin Head books. I recognise your face from the back cover. I've got a few of them.'
'That's me,' Hawk replied. 'I've been called in to work on this case. This is Detective Reeves.' He established from Sid that Charlie had left the pub at about a quarter past eleven, and that there had been just a few other customers in. Locals – Pete and Jackie Wallace, from the bungalow just along the road, first one you came to. They were with a friend, whose name escaped him, used to live in Greatstone. 'Your colleagues went to see the Wallaces yesterday,' Sid ventured. 'They'd know.' No, he'd noticed nothing untoward, just a little banter. Pete and Charlie could both be a bit irritating sometimes, but nothing he hadn't seen before. And Pete would never do anything like that, he was quite sure. It was a terrible, terrible thing. Oh and no, he had not noticed anything strange outside the building either.
Reeves wandered around the room while they talked. The place, with all its treasures, reminded her of her grandmother's front parlour. It was immaculate, but how on earth did a man in a wheelchair keep on top of everything? Presumably, he had help. She paused by a photograph of young pilots – American, judging by the uniforms.
'That will be all for now, thank you, Mr er…?' Hawk looked at Sid enquiringly.
'Sid. Sid Hester. And do come back and sign my books for me sometime, won't you?'
'I'll try.'
Hawk stopped by the door. He pointed to Sid's wheelchair. 'What happened, if you don't mind me asking?'
'Falklands.'

Hawk saluted and followed Reeves down the track to the car. Sid was a funny old stick, he reflected. He couldn't help thinking he had seen him before, though nothing in particular was springing to mind. A pub in the middle of nowhere seemed a strange lifestyle choice and, he agreed with Reeves, it must be difficult to manage. Still, fair play to the guy.
A thought occurred to him. 'Over there is Gratitude Farm, if I remember rightly?' 'Yes, it is,' Reeves replied. 'From The Pumpkin of the Marsh of course. Forensics were there earlier but there's nobody living there. We can drive past if you like.'
As she drove, she tried to remember details of the plot. 'Over by the dyke, as the smugglers' mist swirled, a figure could be discerned…' she began. 'Well remembered,' Hawk laughed. 'Ever seen a smugglers' mist?' Reeves was concentrating as she overtook an old lady on a bicycle. 'Can't say I have,' she replied, 'but I haven't lived down here for all that long.'
Curious about the psychic powers everyone seemed to be talking about, Reeves changed the subject. 'Outside the pub just then, in the road, before we went in, did you…find anything?'
'Elation, then bitter cold,' Hawk replied, enigmatically.
'Couldn't that apply to a lot of places?' she asked. She had read somewhere once that wherever you went, you were walking on bones. History had been her favourite subject at school. Had things been different at home back then, she might have gone further with it.
'Especially back there.' Hawk put his head back and closed his eyes. Reeves turned onto the Burmarsh Road and stopped to let a farmer and six sheep cross the road into their new field.
'He's a strange one,' she thought.

Back in Folkestone later, tactfully turning down Reeves' offer of a nightcap – he was dog tired and it had been an early start - Hawk hit the sack, immediately dropping into a deep sleep. A few hours later, he was woken by a loud buzz from the bedside table. Becky's photo was flashing, as if there was an electric lightbulb behind the glass. The next thing he saw was a figure in black, with a pumpkin for a head, brandishing a knife, coming towards him, closer and closer. Hawk dodged out of the way and the knife went through the pillow. The intruder pulled the knife out and darted out of the door.

Quick as a flash, Hawk ran downstairs after him, mouthing 'thanks, love,' to Becky's photo. He stopped in the hall. Nothing, but the back door was wide open, letting in a blast of cold air. 'Charming,' he murmured. He pulled the door shut and locked it. He went to the kitchen and turned on the kettle and heard a noise in the dining room, as if a large ornament had been disturbed and was rocking on its base. Grabbing a walking stick from the umbrella stand in the hall, Hawk followed the sound. His gaze alighted on an American snowshoe cat, a fine specimen, studiously licking one of its paws. Pippa had explained that snowshoes did not take kindly to being left alone for long periods and that they made their displeasure felt.

'Brian! You gave me a fright!'

Brian regarded him impassively and continued with his ablutions. As Hawk went back through the hall into the kitchen, he could sense something. Over there, in the porch, He spun round. Nothing. Shaking his head, he made himself a cup of tea and found a few treats for Brian.

At the flat in Westbourne Gardens she shared with Patricia, Superintendent Briggs' PA, Detective Constable Reeves was having a pamper night. A bath, with scented candles on the side, and a face mask. Patricia, who was out at a New Folkestone Society Quiz Night, was what Reeves' Mum would have described as a kind soul. Despite being fiercely loyal to Briggs, as was the way of old school PAs, she always kept a watch over the welfare of those under his command. Patricia knew who was worried about an elderly parent, whose wife had just had a baby or who was planning a wedding or a big birthday. She shared in their joys and sorrows alike.

When Reeves had arrived in Folkestone, Patricia had

immediately offered her a place to stay. The offer had been gratefully accepted and, almost a year later, the arrangement still suited them both. As her bath filled, Reeves selected The Black Heart of Blackfriars, the second Mr Pumpkin Head book, from the bookshelf. There must, she thought, if the killer really was shadowing the books, be some link between the victims. She settled into the bath and chose a passage at random.

'Late that night, after all the commuters and revellers had gone to their trains and their beds, a figure walked briskly along the Embankment. It stopped by a steep flight of steps leading down to a wharf and stared down into the black, swirling waters of the Thames, as if seeking inspiration or succour. It clearly found neither. It uttered a tortured cry and then, intoning the words I am he, I am thee, continued on towards Blackfriars.'

Reeves put the book carefully to one side. She knew the story well. The intended victim here was a barrister turned art dealer with the unforgettable moniker of Miles Urbane. He had turned his back on the Bar, and now made his living out of selling what he described as 'Impressionist paintings with a known provenance' at an eye-watering price. An old pupil of his, with whom he had once had an affair, one of many, obligingly churned them out and made up the artists and even gave them a biography. Her parents had forced her to do the Bar conversion course after her degree at the Courtauld, but her heart never lay in the law. Miles operated from an apartment near Blackfriars, which he had owned since his days at the Temple. In the world Dan Hawk had created, some might say that Miles deserved his fate.

She towelled herself dry and put on a bathrobe, and then flicked through the television channels. There was a load of rubbish on every channel -a phrase her Mum would have used. Ivy, Patricia's chihuahua, sat beside her on the sofa. She picked the book up again, as if leafing through it again would yield up clues. O'Neal always said that if you worked your way carefully through the facts, the answer would come. Reeves tended to

be a little too impatient for that sometimes.
Ivy jumped down and stood by the door, growling, hackles raised. 'What's up, girl?'
There was a tentative knock on the door.
'Shit.' Any visitors to the flat had to ring the doorbell outside. That meant that whoever was at the door now was inside the building. Well, the only person who ever knocked on the door was That Arsehole from Nottingham, as Patricia called him, who had snapped up the freehold to all the flats in their building at an auction, outbidding the leaseholders by a slim margin. He had developed a habit of creeping round the building, leaving passive aggressive notes about bins, pushchairs and bicycles in the communal area. He should be in one of Hawk's books, Reeves thought. Perhaps she would suggest it.
'Who is it?' she called. She was bloody well not going to open the door to whoever it was, that was for sure. There was silence. Ivy returned to her perch. Reeves looked out of the window but there was nobody about on the street. She shook her head and picked up a magazine. In the overgrown gardens in the square outside, somebody was staring intently at Reeves' window. They tripped over a bramble bush and cursed roundly and then, with an irritable sigh, clambered over the gate and disappeared into the Folkestone night.
Patricia came home, bearing triumphantly aloft a tin of Quality Street she had won in the raffle. Selecting a green triangle, Reeves ventured:
'What's the story about Hawk and Becky? I know she was killed in a siege a few years ago and nobody really knows why, but what was she like?'
Although she was normally the soul of discretion, a few glasses of Sauvignon at the quiz had loosened Patricia's tongue and she fancied a nightcap She poured herself and Reeves a generous glass of wine from a bottle in the fridge and settled down in the wing-backed armchair she had picked up from the auction house. It suited the room, with its high ceiling and picture rail.

'Becky? She was a lovely girl. She grew up in the West Indies – I can't remember the name of the island offhand, it'll come to me – with her grandparents and then came over here for university. We all went to the wedding. And they'd been married for about three years when it happened. Just thinking about starting a family too.'

Reeves took a swig from her glass. She found Sauvignon and Quality Street rather a peculiar mix, but there was no stopping Patricia now. Not for nothing was she known at the police station as the fount of all knowledge.

'They were great together,' Patricia continued. 'Dan can be a bit difficult at times, as you may have noticed already.' Reeves nodded encouragingly. She stroked Ivy's soft fawn fur as she listened. Patricia leant forwards to select another caramel. 'I have to admit,' she said, as she unwrapped it, 'that I was a little sceptical about his psychic gifts at first. But I really do think there's something in it.'

At Pippa's, Hawk was dead to the world. Brian had come upstairs and was perched at the end of the bed, staring straight at Becky's photo, which was emitting a soft pink glow. Becky shook her head sadly. 'We're going to have to try and look after him, Brian,' she said. 'You and me together.' Brian pulled a claw carefully back from the candlewick bedspread – Pippa went mad if she caught him on any of the beds – and yawned his assent. 'It's getting more and more difficult though,' Becky sighed. 'Good night,' she said, gently.

Sid wheeled himself in through the door of the Shepherd's Hut. He looked smart, in a navy-blue jacket, medals pinned across his chest.

'How was the reunion then, Sid?' Pete called. 'Many there tonight?'

'That's the sad thing.' Sid accepted a small glass of whisky from Fred – always the same routine- and moved over to Pete's table. 'There seem to be fewer of us each time. Way of the world, though, eh? They grow not old and all that. But we carry on, those of us that are left. That's the very least we can do.' His table companions and Fred all raised their glasses in silent tribute. Behind their glass frames, the young soldiers and airmen from an earlier war looked on.

4 RETROSPECT

Gavin Lloyd Goldstein III was standing outside the Excel Centre which was hosting a conference this weekend, different in nature to its usual fare of deathly dull sales conferences and the occasional Arms Fair. 'Comic Con,' the blurb on the sign above him read. 'Where you don't have to be afraid of being YOU!' That, he reflected, was something that has never troubled him. Gavin had played The Cad in a television series of the same name, which ran all the way through the nineties and into the noughties too.

Despite, or perhaps because of, the huge technological advances and social change over recent decades, the British public seemed to have an insatiable appetite for times gone by. Set in the nineteen twenties, the series portrayed Gavin's character – The Cad - as a chancer, trying his luck in the most exquisite of locations, from the casinos of Montreux and Monte Carlo to the stately homes of England and back, via Paris, to the villas of Cap d'Antibes. Following in the footsteps of the Hemingways and the Fitzgeralds, The Cad would always redeem himself by taking on and defeating an even more outrageous cad than himself. Each episode would end with Gavin making a discreet exit in his Bentley, sweeping through the gates of whichever exotic place he was in, just before any awkward questions were raised by his hosts. In the background as the credits rolled, and the theme tune, 'I'll drink your champagne' played, would be Dopey Doris the parlour maid, always looking dumbstruck at the antics of her employers and The Cad. The series catchphrase was 'Bloody Bounders!' which was clever, as it left viewers wondering which of the characters were the Bounders.

Gavin's father, God rest his soul, had been a shrewd business man and had made sure the deal the television studios did with his imbecile of a son (his words) gave Gavin most of the rights over merchandise. 'Can't think there would be much of that,' a patronising executive had remarked. They rued their decision when the series, the theme tune, the catchphrase, and the black bowler hat Gavin always wore took on iconic status. Gavin's father bought a small Provençal vineyard and came up with a Bloody Bounders label. It proved immensely popular; people could (and to Gavin's amazement still did) go on Bloody Bounders-themed holidays and cruises. He left that side of things to his mother, who had moved to Provence, while he continued with a sybaritic lifestyle in London.

'Don't mind me,' Gavin muttered, as he was almost knocked flying by two Spidermen, an Orc and an Incredible Hulk, all chatting animatedly. He gave a tut of annoyance and lit another cigarette. He did not like being kept waiting. Not one bit. Then, Ross Norman from Five at Five hurtled past. 'Finally,' he commented, looking ostentatiously at his watch, as Ross came to a skittering halt in front of him.

'Gavin, so sorry, got held up. Let's get started, shall we?' She started talking right away. Gavin hurriedly put out his cigarette. 'Good morning. I'm Ross Norman, live from Comic Con, and I have here with me this morning Gavin Lloyd Goldstein. The news was leaked last week that Gavin would be playing Mr Pumpkin Head in the movie franchise of the same name. How do you feel?'

Gavin almost purred. 'What can I say? Perfect casting. The role I was born to play. It's very exciting…'

Ross cut in. 'But don't you think it's dreadful, about this person dressing up as the person you are going to play and MURDERING people?'

Gavin brushed her aside. 'Well, it certainly wasn't me, folks. Now, I might be 'method,' but I don't need to kill someone in real life to know what it feels like. That, my dear, is what is called acting, as I once told Bobby de Niro.'

Ross's eyes were beginning to glaze over. Who the hell did this conceited old has-been think he was, anyway? Her interview with Superman was coming up any time now and she was bloody well not going to lose her slot. She decided to ignore what was coming out of her earpiece.

'Is this your comeback after The Cad?'

'I never went away, my dear.'
'Oh yes, tell us about those beer commercials, Gavin. Are you still drinking the profits?'
'Let's not dwell on the past. I'm so thrilled to be in my first movie…'
'Would you call yourself an actor's actor?'
'One day,' Gavin said, deciding not to play up to the daft trollop, 'I hope to utter those famous words, spoken by the late, great Alan Swan. I'm not an actor. I'm a movie star.'
The producer was screaming CUT so loudly into Ross's ear that even Gavin could hear it. 'Thank you, Gavin,' Ross said. 'This is Ross Norman for Five at Five. Live from Comic Con. And now…'
Gavin stalked off in the direction of Tower Bridge. Nothing, but nothing, and least of all her, was going to spoil his triumph. Now, where, in this God-forsaken part of the metropolis, was there a decent pub for a self-respecting Cad to get a pint? A couple in identical red cagoules came towards him. 'Bloody Bounders,' they chorused. 'Oh, fuck off,' he retorted. It was worth it every time, just to see the crushed expression on their faces. 'And you can fuck off too,' he told a pigeon, as it flew into the air in a flash of grey and green, having narrowly escaped the toe of his highly polished boot.

In his room at Pippa's, Hawk watched the car crash of an interview with the man who was going to play Mr Pumpkin Head. He turned the television off in disgust and headed over to Chambers. O'Neal had suggested they meet there again today, as 'Super' Briggs had told him that he would prefer it if they met off the premises for the time being.
Sensing he was rattled, Reeves went over and ordered Hawk's tea for him. 'You ok, Detective?' she asked quietly.
'I've been better.' Hawk gave her a smile. He told them about last night's visitation. 'Starting to wish I'd never written those bloody Mr Pumpkin Head books though. Perhaps I should have written psychic books instead or stuck to history.'
'Speaking of which,' said O'Neal, 'I'm not trying to doubt you

but if you were psychic, would you not have sensed the danger?'
'There's one reason – and one reason only – why my psychic ability hasn't kicked in.' Hawk paused. 'It's because we're not looking for a ghost. This person is real.'
'But then why hasn't anybody been able to find fingerprints?' asked O'Neal.
'There must be a rational explanation.' Hawk sipped at his tea. 'As this isn't a psychic matter, do you want me off the case?'
'No way. You're involved now.' O'Neal was adamant. He might be sceptical about the psychic side of things, but Hawk had always had a sound reputation. It was good to have him on board. 'Would you like me to send a patrol car up to Pippa's at night, in case he tries again?'
'Tries to kill you,' Reeves added helpfully.
Hawk shook his head. 'I think this person is trying to scare me. Of course, he or she has now killed three people. Technically, that makes them a serial killer. We need to find out why.'
'It's almost as if,' Reeves looked pensive 'we have to wait until he kills again.' She thought about mentioning her nocturnal visitor but decided against it; it could after all only have been That Arsehole from Nottingham.
Hawk pushed back his chair. 'Let's go,' he said. 'Back to Pippa's. Nobody else booked in and she's away. We'll set up an Ops Room there.'

Pippa's dining room was soon transformed. A large board was positioned against the wall, full of notes and photographs. Reeves had started putting it together back at the station. She stood back to admire her handiwork, almost treading on Brian, who was most put out by all this activity and in the middle of the day too. He stalked out into the hallway in high dudgeon, the tip of his tail twitching slightly.
'If the murderer is following my book tour,' Hawk began, 'presumably they will stay near Folkestone, as I am here.' He stared at the victims' details, as if seeking inspiration.
Beverley Smithe – Peterborough Cathedral

John Carlton Jones – London Dungeon
Charlie Green – Romney Marsh, not far from the Shepherd's Hut.

Dan and Reeves told O'Neal about their visit to the pub yesterday. 'Landlord's a real history buff, 'Reeves reported. 'You couldn't get another picture on those walls if you tried.'

It was a shame, they all remarked, that the footage from the London Dungeon was so indistinct. It had simply picked up the crowd scenes. However, a passer-by had reported seeing a figure in black robes, with a pumpkin for a head, exiting the back of the building, and James, one of the victim's pupils, had testified to seeing the figure in the crowd. The Met had been up and down the neighbouring streets, asking people for footage from their Ring doorbells. Again, nothing much doing.

'Just this. It isn't very good.' O'Neal showed them grainy footage of a male, about 5 foot 8, a baseball cap pulled over his brow, on the corner behind the Dungeon, turning down one of the narrow back streets, towards a derelict warehouse. After that, the camera lost him. 'Can't really tell much from that,' Hawk commented. 'Although what's that he's carrying? A rucksack of some kind?'

'Probably some geezer on his way to the gym.' O'Neal was dismissive. All the same, Reeves made a careful note on the board about a male, around five foot 8 with baseball cap and rucksack and, by Charlie's name, she wrote 'Elation and bitter cold.' She added a question mark.

There must, Hawk voiced his thoughts aloud, be some connection between the victims rather than them being random targets. A teacher, a mum and an eighties television star. What could link them?

'It's just that if the killer really is following my books, you would say that the victims deserved their fate. In the series, Mr Pumpkin Head is a kind of vigilante. A force for the good. Arguably, anyway.' He gazed into space. 'And I'm just not getting that impression, not so far, anyway.'

'We haven't got very much on the victims yet. I'll do some more work on the profiling,' Reeves volunteered.

Suddenly, Hawk's mobile rang. 'Superintendent Briggs,' he mouthed, to his colleagues. 'OK, I'll be with you in ten.'

'Want a lift?' Reeves led the way out to the car. O'Neal got in the front and Hawk in the back, and within moments they were at the police station again. This morning, it hadn't hit home that he was back on his old stomping ground, a few minutes' walk from his and Becky's old flat. This time it did, with a vengeance. The memories…He took the stairs two at a time. Old habits died hard. Briggs was standing by the window, looking out.

'You do know you're only working on this case because O'Neal convinced me to let you?' Briggs started on Hawk straightaway.

'I'm very well, thank you, how are you?' Hawk was in a take no prisoners mood.

'Don't take that tone with me. I'm giving you the chance to right the wrong of writing those bloody books. And on your own patch too. 'In Folkestone, they do things differently,' indeed. For God's sake, Hawk. You know better than that, surely?'

Hawk cut in. 'Do you think I would have written them if I had thought for one moment that some lunatic was going to start slaughtering people?'

'I don't know, is the answer to that. All I can say is that there are cops in this building, and elsewhere too, right now who would kill to be running a case like this. Some of them, I might add, may be a tad pissed off when word gets out that you're back.'

'Oh yes? Might I enquire who they are?' Hawk snorted. Divide and rule had always been Briggs' mantra. Anyone with half a braincell could see right through him. It was pathetic really.

'Well, Detectives Tyronne, Edge and Sellers and that's just for starters. Even PC Jackson said he might take a crack at the case if he could. And there's old Coogan too, looking for a swansong. Not to mention his sidekick, Elise Palmer.' Briggs paused. The litany of names was having no effect on Hawk. 'Look, all I want is results. Go out there and get some. If you reckon you are capable of that?'

'As long as I don't listen to you,' Hawk shot back, 'I'll be fine. I have nothing else to lose this time.'

Briggs looked away. That remark was below the belt, but he had to admit, probably well-deserved. He poured himself a glass of water and sat down at his desk. His mind went back to that night – how the years had flashed past. They'd all been busy at the station – nothing new there – with the Isobel Entwhistle case, the new landlady at the Unicorn whose tenure had been brutally cut short. He, and indeed his predecessor, had always described that place as a nest of vipers. They'd rounded up the usual suspects. Nothing.

Isobel's killing had caused a right palaver. It had been pointed out to him - forcefully – that desperately-needed new investment was hardly likely to flood into Folkestone if swathes of it provided a haven for lowlifes, drug addicts and criminals. You could have all the Triennials, fancy restaurants and art schools you wanted, but if people didn't feel safe on the streets, they wouldn't want to buy property there. All very well, he'd thought at the time, but resources were so thin on the ground. In the end, he'd agreed that there might be some merit in Hawk's suggestion that Isobel's problems could have followed her to Folkestone. He'd sent him up to her old patch in West London. 'Use the old psychic powers,' he'd said, with a wry smile. 'Throw everything at it.'

That morning, a dossier had appeared on his desk, passed on from the Met, about a certain Bob Collins, who had moved into the area, and taken up again with an old girlfriend, Avelyn Walter. The Met enquiry, which was then still ongoing, had been given the name 'Syndicate' and his counterpart at the Met had said, over the telephone, that they'd wanted Briggs to know that these characters had moved into his manor. He hadn't read the dossier straightaway or even skimmed through it – he'd left early for an appointment with his masseuse – but the gist of it was that Bob was a blackmailer and an extortionist in his own right, with links with some very unsavoury people. A couple of years back, footage had emerged of Bob and

Avelyn on a Russian oligarch's floating gin palace. Bob had been convicted of firearms offences not long afterwards and had recently been released from gaol. Avelyn was also known to the police, although not only because of her association with Bob. Formerly an upmarket escort, she had served time for various related misdemeanours. Saying that, nothing much had been pinned on her in recent times.

'Nasty piece of work all the same, 'his counterpart had explained. 'As for Bob, now that we've got him housed, we'd like a close eye kept.'

'If only,' Briggs thought, 'I'd rearranged that massage appointment and sat and read that dossier.' All right, life was full of 'if only stories' but the consequences of some decisions were devastating. Back at the station later that afternoon, a call had come in from Avelyn's neighbour in Turketel Road, reporting an altercation. The woman seemed more concerned about the decline of the neighbourhood; she'd ranted on about it for several moments.

'Could you make out what was being said at all?' The desk officer had apparently tapped her pen on her notepad, no doubt looking forward to the end of a boring shift.

'Absolutely disgraceful…my husband and I rue the day they put that High-Speed line in…oh, it's useful all right, used it a few times myself, but I said all along it would attract all sorts of riffraff and now look…What's that you say? Oh yes, a female – I think it was HER – said something like 'the same thing as happened to Isobel.' The nice girl who does the garden is there (Becky, I think her name is) no, she isn't the one shouting, and someone else, another woman, no, never seen her before. No, it's gone quiet now; this was an hour ago. the car's not there. Whose car? I don't know. It could be that bloke of hers. Don't like him either. You'll look into it? Well, I should bloody well hope so, wondering why we bother paying our rates…'

The desk officer had gone back to her copy of Hello, with a cup of tea and a nice digestive biscuit. She had casually mentioned the call to O'Neal after the end of her shift, having sat and watched the minute hand on the clock going round.

O'Neal had stopped in his tracks. 'Isobel?' he'd said. 'Wait. Isn't that the woman who was killed at the Unicorn? Where did you say the call came from? What time? And you didn't see fit to mention it before?'

It wasn't long after that, Briggs recalled, that Hawk had stormed in. He'd had a brief call from Becky. 'Dan, I need help,' she'd said, before her phone battery died. Briggs had tried to calm Hawk down, told him he'd sent a patrol car round, that it was probably nothing, that the neighbour had said that things had quietened down now, and anyway, why would Avelyn want to harm Becky?

'Because,' Hawk had said, in that way he had sometimes, as if he was talking to an idiot, 'they'll have heard that I've been on their old patch today, making enquiries about Isobel. And Isobel was involved in their little cartel. Up to her neck; that pub business was just a front, same as Avelyn's PR. Look, she and Collins have offices in Tontine Street. I'm sure that's where they've got Becky.'

It was to his eternal shame, Briggs reflected, that he'd repeated that the patrol car was on its way to Turketel Road. If it really was a hostage situation, then they would have heard from the hostage takers by now. Worse still, he'd told Hawk to put the psychic crap on hold and get on with some proper policing. Hawk had slammed out of his office and got straight into his car. Briggs had caught up and he went with him to prove the point. Blue light flashing, siren on, they got to Turketel Road before the patrol car. Hawk's instinct had been correct. It was the wrong place, and although they dashed straight round to Tontine Street, again on a wing and a prayer, they were too late. Poor girl. Briggs hadn't seen the blow that Hawk landed on him coming, but to use the vernacular, he'd gone down like a sack of shit. It was a strange thing, he reflected, but to this day nobody had ever fathomed the full extent of what had gone on that night and whether there had been anyone else lurking in the background. Bob's alibi seemed to have been strong; he'd been at the hospital that evening at his elderly father's bedside. Avelyn had gone down for both killings –

Isobel's and Becky's too. A siege situation that went too far; still, an awful business.

The telephone on Briggs' desk rang, waking him from his slumber. He looked up – he must have been asleep for ages, it was dark. 'Briggs here. What? Where? What did they say again? Oh, for fuck's sake. Well? What are you waiting for? Get Hawk and O'Neal down there straightaway.'

His head was throbbing. He poured himself a glass of water and sat quietly for a moment. Any ideas he might have entertained about a steady run down to retirement and maybe even a special award were now vanishing fast. He stared at the blood trickling from his hands and realised that his glass had shattered. With his good hand, he picked up the phone again and summoned Patricia. 'Better bring the first aid kit,' he said.

5 BESIEGED

John Reece lurched forward and gripped the handrail with both hands as he made his unsteady way down the steps from the top deck of the no. 16. The last bus, and he'd caught it by the skin of his teeth. He gave the driver a cheerful wave as he stepped off at his stop. Several hours of carousing with college friends in Canterbury, in the Thomas Ingoldsby, had taken their toll. All the same, landing a part in a London play – with Jed Cabot no less – was worthy of a celebration and it had been good to see everyone. Now that his parents had passed away, there was nobody left in Folkestone for him to celebrate with and nothing much to keep him there. Perhaps a move was on the cards.

His road had thus far escaped gentrification. In the surrounding streets, the houses all had skips parked outside and seemed constantly to be festooned with scaffolding. On his road, the houses still had front gardens, a haven for small birds. He liked that and leaving his little garden would certainly be a wrench, although he did need to get out there and do some cutting back. It had been his late mother's domain and had become very overgrown.

It was very dark – more overgrown trees opposite had long since obscured the only street lamp and the Council was deaf to residents' complaints. Somebody was making their way along on the other side of the road – a woman in a headscarf, a rucksack on her back. She turned into Mrs. Turner's at number 37; funny, he thought Mrs. Turner lived on her own. She hadn't been very well; he sometimes offered to pick up shopping for her. She always let him keep the change. Perhaps it was a new carer; they did tend to come and go. He waved to the woman and she raised a gloved hand in salute.

As John walked up the path, he could hear his television. He had got into the habit, since he had been on his own, of leaving it on when he went out. Walking into a silent house was just grim. As he took his key out of his pocket, he spotted

a pound coin on the path. He stooped to pick it up. A figure loomed in front of him.
'What the fuck do you want?' John straightened up and glared at the apparition, in black robes with a pumpkin mask.
'Well, it isn't trick or treat. I want your key.' The voice that came out of the mask, with a slight London inflection, seemed faintly ridiculous.
'Fuck off,' John responded and received a punch in his face. The figure opened the door with his key. His own front door. His haven! How dare he? He followed the figure inside. 'Now look here!' His copy of Acting Up Weekly was on the hall table, just where he had left it earlier. He grabbed it. It might just do; better than nothing. Over in the corner was his Mum's old walking stick, if he could only reach it, but the figure whipped round and pushed him down onto his knees and slit his throat. He had the curious sensation as he drifted in and out of consciousness, of his forehead being written on, with something sharp. Then, was he imagining it, he saw the woman with the headscarf and rucksack he'd spotted before, running out of the door? What the actual…but the images in his brain now resembled those he used to see in his toy kaleidoscope. He crawled slowly and painfully towards the front room, magazine still in his hand.

'What time do you call this?' In the small hours of the morning, Hawk was standing outside Pippa's, jacket slung over his shoulder, as O'Neal drew up. Brian, returning from a hunting expedition, weaved in and out of his legs before disappearing round the back of the house.
'Hop in.' O'Neal opened the passenger door. 'Didn't want to say too much on the phone, but I had a call – somebody rang the station and said they spotted a person in a pumpkin mask in the Radnor Park area late yesterday evening. Could just be kids, I suppose, but it's a bit early yet for trick or treating.' Dan put his seatbelt on. 'Let's go and have a look. Who was it that phoned?'
'That's the strange thing,' O'Neal replied. 'They wouldn't give

their name. But before they hung up, they said I am He, I am thee.'

'That's a quote from my books,' said Hawk.

'Weird or what? Anyway, we're here now. Now, one thing they did mention was number 46.' O'Neal parked the car and they started walking down a small road of Edwardian houses; many had been converted into flats. There was a lamp post at one end of the road. but the trees had grown up round it, so it hardly gave any light. 'This one.' Hawk nudged O'Neal. The door to number 46 was wide open. As they crept through the hall, they could hear the television. They nodded to each other and went in.

There was a film on. Every Dog has its Day. It was a gangster movie, shot in that retro way that was so popular nowadays, lots of dark interiors, lingering camera shots and strange angles. As Hawk's old nan would have said, 'I can't hear a bloody word half of them are saying.' Lee Trickett, however, was playing the lead villain, one Phil Garland. Nan would have had no trouble with his enunciation.

'Lee Trickett's a local lad, isn't he?' Hawk asked. 'I do like his films. I wish…Jesus Christ, what's that?' He pointed at a mangled, bloody heap on a green Persian rug, just as Trickett came out with the line: 'You could say I'm not having a very good day.'

'Well, that's perfect timing,' O'Neal commented. Hawk knelt beside the body. 'Dead as a doornail, poor sod. Been here a good couple of hours, I reckon. Strange none of the neighbours noticed the door was open but then again it's quite overgrown at the front.' O'Neal came over. 'I see Mr Pumpkin Head has had his carving set out again.' True to form, the word 'NEXT!' was inscribed on the victim's forehead. They stood for a moment, looking down at him, as Trickett barked out an order from the television: 'Just get rid of him, will you?' O'Neal shook his head. 'He's coming out with all the lines tonight, isn't he?'

'Fuck, there's somebody here.' Hawk and O'Neal whirled round to face the intruder, who had a gun drawn.

'Didn't I just tell you to fuck off?' snarled Trickett from the television.

'Well, that's a nice welcome, I must say,' Reeves observed. 'I heard about the mystery call and thought I'd come and have a look-see.'

She spotted the body on the floor. 'Oh God, not another one. I'll call in now.'

By the time they had handed over to Forensics, the birds in the trees nearby were starting to sing, and there was a faint glimmer of dawn. Satisfied that all was as well as it could be, Reeves had gone home an hour before. Hawk was silent in the car going back to Pippa's, as if deep in thought. 'Penny for them.' O'Neal prodded him. 'Getting any of those psychic vibes?' Hawk shook his head. 'Wish it was as simple as that. Night.'

Hawk made himself a cup of tea to take up with him. Brian walked regally up the stairs in front of him, as if rather glad of the company. As he kicked off his shoes and lay down on top of the bed, he looked over at Becky's photo. 'Love you,' he whispered. Tonight though, Becky was keeping her counsel. Thoughts were jumping around in his head. His books had been out for a few years so why now? In them, the victims – some would say – deserved their fate. That wasn't the case here, surely. He started to go over all the murder scenes in his mind. Katharine of Aragon's Tomb, the London Dungeon and halfway down a drovers' track on the Romney Marsh. He had visited the tomb in Peterborough Cathedral a few times, and he began mentally to retrace his steps, before drifting into a troubled sleep.

Roderick Sadler, the owner of the Sun and Surf Café, had come to Folkestone to live the dream, having taken early retirement from a merchant bank. A Londoner born and bred, and proud of it, Roderick had spent a few childhood summer holidays in Cornwall, and had loved the little coves, the golden sands and the blue skies. The pay-off from the bank had been good, but not that good, and so he'd decided on Folkestone instead which, all the broadsheets told him, was a happening place.

He'd taken over the lease from what had been a fish and chip shop, a short walk from the Harbour, next to an art gallery. He'd immediately set about stripping it back, painting it in dazzling whites and vibrant blues. He had spent a bomb on Cornish blue pottery, and in every inglenook, there were miniature lighthouses and cottages. Sun and Surf had opened with a fanfare. As the summer turned into autumn though, things had quietened right down. He'd come down to look at the place in June, on a stunning Sunday when the beach was packed, and crowds were flocking to the Harbour Arm. A grim winter Monday would probably have given him a more realistic idea. The gallery next door scarcely seemed to open.

Something else he hadn't bargained for was the physical hard grind of running a café. His wife had made it clear she was not remotely interested in helping. He had quickly hired staff – a chef to come up with attractive menus to attract the punters and, as a waiter and general factotum, Adam, who was eighteen and had decided not to join the annual exodus of school leavers to university. Gloria came in most mornings, before she had to pick her grandchildren up from playgroup, to help with breakfasts. They were all good workers – the punters loved Gloria and her slightly grumpy demeanour as much as Adam, who always remembered how everyone liked their coffee and had endless patience and friendly advice for those who struggled to make their minds up. That said, if things didn't pick up soon, he might have to cut their hours back. If he could only get through the first winter, that would be a major hurdle. Saying that, this morning wasn't too bad so far, customer-wise.

Two ladies had just come in and were looking through the menu (recently revamped and presented neatly in a folder.) At a table by the window, a man in an old donkey jacket that had seen better days was flicking through the local paper. A picture from the cover of Dan Hawk's first book, The Pumpkin of the Marsh, was on the front page. He'd been one of the first in this morning and, after a full English breakfast, was spinning out his cups of tea. Adam had been over a couple of times to ask if he wanted anything else. It looked as if he was waiting for somebody.

Local poet and tour guide Tony Quarrington came in to order takeaway teas, coffees and pastries for a group on one of his literary tours. They were at the halfway point and in need of sustenance. One of the tour members, Pamela, an aspiring writer, had joined him in the queue with her daughter, who was down for the weekend. Roderick waved to them all. He always liked it when the 'creatives' came in.

'That's two Earl Greys, one with lemon please, Gloria,' said Tony. An English Breakfast but not too strong. Two lattes and four cappuccinos – one of them with oat milk. And – what was that, Pam? Oh yes, four almond croissants and four plain.'

A black Bentley Continental drew up across the road and a tall man wearing an expensive suit got out, carefully avoiding sullying his Jermyn Street brogues with the dog shit that – despite countless and vociferous complaints from Roderick, the gallery owner next door and residents – still festooned the street. Roderick watched as the man turned to his chauffeur.

'It's all right, Jon, I'll get it myself this time. I could do with a little break. I'm sure you can find yourself something useful to do for half an hour? Good man.'

'Here comes trouble,' Roderick chuckled, as Arthur Montgomery approached. They always had a nice chat about business, the races and Folkestone's rising fortunes. He turned to Adam. 'Let me guess – he'll go for an avocado and tomato sandwich on rye, with just a dash of tabasco sauce. Washed down with a flat white with an extra shot.'

'He can wait his turn.' Gloria was preoccupied, making up Tony's order. 'I never queue, my dear,' said Montgomery, as he walked towards the counter. Adam stepped in. 'The usual, sir?' he enquired. Before Montgomery could respond, the man at the table stood up, drew out a gun and pointed it at him. 'It's a stick-up!'

Hawk had made his way down to Sunny Sands, past the Unicorn, which still had a For Sale sign outside, and along the Stade. It had become part of his pre-work circuit. Dogs were allowed on the Sands again, now that summer was over. He and Becky had discussed getting a dog; probably would have done. He stood for a moment in the sunshine and watched two puppies racing each other for a ball, as they dashed in and out of the waves. Their exuberance and sheer joie de vivre made him smile. A couple of preschoolers dashed in and out of the arches, playing hide and seek, while their mothers chatted. After the years of Covid lockdown which, he had been told, had been particularly grim in Kent, it was good to see people out and enjoying themselves.

His mobile rang. Briggs yet again. Now what?

'Hawk,' Briggs began. 'Sorry to disturb, but we have a hostage situation in town.'

Hawk sighed. 'Do you not have anyone else who could cover it?'

'That's the thing. The hostage-taker has asked for you specifically. You should be flattered. He must have heard that you were back in town.'

'It's not Mr Pumpkin Head then?' Hawk queried.

'He didn't say it was. He didn't give a name when he rang. It's just the hostage and the hostage-taker – he let the owner and the staff go, and the other customers. Thank goodness, as there were a few of them. A young girl, Tina, rang in just now too – said she was on a literary tour with her Mum!'

'That'll give them all something to write home about. Do we know who the hostage is?'

'Yes,' Briggs replied. 'Local businessman Arthur Montgomery. You might remember him. Anyway, they're at the Sun and Surf Café in Tontine Street. You'd probably remember it as the chippy.'

Hawk retraced his footsteps along the Stade. Everyone had heard of Arthur Montgomery. Even if they had never met him, they talked about him as though they had. Even so, he made a call to Reeves, to get a little extra background on the man. She

was happy to oblige. 'Much appreciated,' he commented. 'This could be interesting.'
'Oh, and there's a way in to the café around the back,' Reeves added. 'Takes you in past the Ladies.'
As Hawk neared the café, he decided to take Reeves's advice and doubled back down a side street. A patrol car drew up beside him. Good, some back-up – PC Jackson and a new copper he didn't recognise. Giving them a thumbs up, he went in through the back of the café, and paused for a moment in the corridor. There was a glass panel in the door leading into the main part of the café, through which he could see the hostage-taker facing the street entrance. He had a gun to Montgomery's head.
'And just who the hell are you?' Montgomery drawled. 'I presume you know who I am.'
'Why do you think you have a gun in your ear?' came the response. 'Doesn't matter who I am.'
'And who are you waiting for?'
'Detective, slash writer, Dan Hawk.'
'Now look here, I must warn you,' began Montgomery, but the hostage-taker, tightening his grip on his gun, hissed: 'I don't want your money. I just want Hawk here.' They made an incongruous pair, Hawk reflected, as the hostage-taker was only five foot six. Still, the idiot could do some damage with the .38 revolver he was holding, and this was his cue. He pushed the door open and appeared behind them. 'Turn around,' he ordered.
The hostage-taker and Montgomery complied.
'Hawk,' said the hostage-taker. 'You took your fucking time.'
'Do I know you?' Hawk asked.
'No, but you knew my girlfriend, Avelyn Walter. She killed your wife, remember? Name's Bob Collins.'
Now he remembered the name. That lowlife. Briggs had been sent a dossier on him. If he recalled rightly – it had all been such a blur – he'd been on some sort of watch list. Briggs, true to form, hadn't bothered to read it. Anyway, he was fully prepared now to tear Collins limb from limb. Montgomery

meanwhile had begun to tire of this. He spoke up. 'Look, what does all this have to do with me?'

'Glad you asked,' came the response. 'Hawk, if Avelyn is not released from prison, I am going to blow this fine gentleman away.'

'You might want to rethink that,' Hawk advised. He gave an almost imperceptible nod to PC Jackson, who was outside in the corridor. 'You see, what most people don't know about Arthur Montgomery is that he is ex Special Forces. As if on cue, Montgomery, in one swift move grabbed Collins by the wrist and disarmed him. Collins doubled up in agony as Montgomery twisted his wrist.

'I did try to warn you.' Montgomery shrugged, as PC Jackson moved forwards and snapped the cuffs on Collins. 'Anyway, all I came in for was an avocado and tomato sandwich on rye. With a splash of tabasco sauce. And a flat white with an extra shot. Shop!' He rang the bell on the counter as if expecting Roderick, Gloria and Adam to materialise.

'I'll get the staff back in,' said Hawk. 'I'm sure it will be on the house.'

Montgomery sat down to wait at the table Collins had been occupying. He picked up the newspaper and looked at the front page. Pumpkin terror in Folkestone, the headline screamed. 'Dear oh dear,' he murmured. 'Hope they catch this bastard too,' he called, as PC Jackson dragged Collins, none too gently, round to the front of the café and into the waiting patrol car.

Back at the police station, Hawk decided to leave them all to it and, after a brief conversation with Briggs, made his excuses. 'I just wouldn't trust myself.' 'Do you think the two incidents are connected?' Briggs asked. 'Bob Collins and this Pumpkin Head psycho?' 'I don't think so,' Hawk replied. Reeves and O'Neal were waiting for him downstairs. 'Beers are on you later,' they chorused. 'Round yours.'

Hawk took the scenic route back to Pippa's, along the Leas. He stopped by the bandstand, where Tony was reading to his

group from a letter Wilfred Owen had written to his mother in January 1917 about his stay in Folkestone. He'd put up at the best hotel, he wrote, where the carpets were as deep as the mud in France, there were golden flunkeys and even the porters had clean hands. He stood and listened.
'Now,' Tony concluded, 'it's often been said that anything can happen on one of Tony's tours, and it usually does. I didn't have an armed hold-up in mind, though! Thanks, everyone and see you again soon.'
Hawk gave the group a friendly wave. These literary types were obviously made of stern stuff. He walked on towards the Road of Remembrance and, on the way down, paused to read the panel with Carol Duffy's poem. 'Down the quiet road,' it began. It was good, he reflected, that the road, often one of the last sights of Blighty for soldiers going to the Front, was being looked after now.

When he got back to his room, he straightened Becky's photo frame. She looked out at him sadly. 'You know, it won't bring me back, Dan.' Was it his imagination, he wondered, or did her voice seem slightly fainter, as if she had moved further away? He had asked her the other day whether she had found her grandparents. 'Not yet. But I'm hoping to, soon,' the reply had been. That had surprised him. He would have thought they would have been her very first port of call, on an island like the one where she had grown up. He tried again tonight.
'What's it like then, Becks, on the other side?'
She sighed. 'I can't describe it, Dan. It's nothing like you would ever imagine. And things aren't straightforward here; they're not linear. You don't just get to make your way wherever you please and whenever for that matter. Or with just anybody. Oh, it's so hard to explain. Look, I've got to go…'
'Go? Where? Wait!' but it was no good. With a sigh, Hawk went back downstairs and headed out to the off-licence in search of supplies for the evening and, crucially, more cat treats for Brian.

Hawk and Reeves sat in Pippa's living room, with a beer each, while O'Neal took a call outside. It had been quite a day. Even Brian seemed exhausted. Reeves stroked him under the chin, which he accepted gracefully before jumping onto an armchair, where he proceeded to clean his whiskers. Dan smiled. 'Blimey. You're honoured. Pippa told me he doesn't usually like ladies very much. Apart from her, that is.'

O'Neal put his mobile back in his pocket and came and joined them for a beer. The name of last night's victim, he told them, was John Reece. Forensics had now confirmed what they had suspected – that the victim didn't die straightaway and had managed to crawl into the living room, holding a rolled-up magazine which he had probably intended to use as a weapon. The cause of death was the same. A cut to the throat and the word NEXT! carved on his forehead. However, this time, a fragment of the murder weapon was stuck in the victim's forehead. Now, they had to wait for the post-mortem results.

Hawk closed his eyes. He was struggling to understand, and he voiced his thoughts to his companions, why the murders had started to happen in the past week and what had triggered them.

'A crazy fan?' O'Neal ventured. 'Maybe somebody jealous of your success?'

'But which fan?' Reeves looked round at them. She had been adding some notes about this latest victim to the board. Younger than the other victims, living alone. Recently lost his mother, according to the neighbours. She underlined his age – twenty-five – with a green marker pen. That explained why he had put up a fight.

'I'm just wondering,' Hawk began, 'whether it has something to do with the film rights being leaked. That was about a week ago. I wouldn't say it was headline news, but I've a hunch that someone may have taken note.' He turned to O'Neal and Reeves. 'How about I do another book signing? It might just flush them out.'

O'Neal was unsure. 'I don't know. It could end up as a real bloodbath.'

'Listen,' Hawk was on a roll. 'I do the same bookshop as before – Marrins. Perhaps late afternoon. You place a surveillance team strategically around it. Any sign of Mr Pumpkin Head and you guys can be in there like a shot.'
'I'm not convinced.' O'Neal frowned. 'I have to say I don't like it and Briggs will like it even less.'
'Briggs,' Hawk replied, 'wants results. He told me that himself.'
O'Neal thought for a moment. That feeling of unease was still there. Maybe there was something in this psychic nonsense after all. All the same, Hawk was right; drastic action was needed. 'I'll set it up,' he said. 'We're going to mash this Pumpkin!'
'On that note,' Reeves stood up. 'I'll see you tomorrow, guys.'

Later, Hawk dialled Vic Barkley's number.
'How's it going?'
'Couldn't be better,' Vic replied. It was that time of year when putting the heating on was tempting. Vic, however, was a Spartan. Many said of him that he was old before his time. He sat at his desk in coat, hat and gloves. 'I was away for a couple of days -just got back. Book sales, old boy, are going through the roof! How are things down in Midsomer?'
'Don't joke. He's killed again and almost killed me the other night.'
'Can't have that,' Vic shot back. 'Not until we've got a few more books under our belt.' He glanced at the framed prints of Hawk's books, on the wall opposite him.
'I love the royal we, Vic. You'll be glad to know that I'm doing another book signing tomorrow. Same place – Marrins in Folkestone…'
Vic was positively bubbling over. 'You know Gavin Goldstein is set to play Mr Pumpkin Head?'
'Yes, worse luck. You told me the other day. Comes to something, when that's the best they can come up with! What next, a cameo role for Dopey Doris? I've heard of scraping the barrel, Vic, but this takes the biscuit. If you'll excuse the mixed metaphor.'

Vic ignored him. 'Goldstein is itching to get back on the publicity trail. Why don't I send him down? Great publicity.'
Dan plucked at a thread on his sleeve. This could be dangerous. Although he had never met the man, Goldstein's reputation went before him. From what the newspapers said, he'd been pissed ever since the nineties. He could be a liability. Vic himself was a loose cannon, and probably the less he knew about the operation the better. Then again, if Goldstein was there, things might seem more normal, and Reeves and O'Neal were sorting out a surveillance team. 'All right,' he conceded.
'That's settled; I'll get the film company to put him on the train tomorrow morning. Tata for now' Vic put the telephone down. This could, with any luck, be the break he and indeed all literary agents always dreamt of. A writer whose books just sold themselves and a film (hopefully the first of several) coming out; Dan was right on the cusp. Maybe – just maybe - he could allow himself to think about moving out of this freezing dump at last. 'I'm good,' he sang. 'Bloody damn good.'

6 SIGNING

At the police station, the air of excitement was almost tangible as preparations for Hawk's book signing got underway. Reeves was in her element. It had been a while since she'd been involved in anything quite like this. It reminded her of her days at the Met. Briggs had been as good as his word and extra resources had been drafted in. She looked round. DS O'Neal had finished his part of the briefing and was on his mobile phone. He gave her an encouraging nod.

'Now,' she said, to the assembled team. 'Anybody got any questions? Coogan and Palmer, you'll man the fort here. Detective Black? Detective White? You're in the advance party with me. Everything clear?'

You couldn't make it up., she thought. Detective Black and Detective White. Mick White was tall and powerfully built, and despite years of living and working in Kent, had not lost his Dublin accent. Keith Black had dreamt, growing up in Cheshire, of becoming a policeman, but had been told that he would not be tall enough. When the rules changed, he'd joined straightaway, aged eighteen and five foot seven in his socks. He'd moved down to Folkestone many years ago with his girlfriend, now his wife. He and White made a great duo. Some, rather unkindly, said that Black and White, the name by which they were jointly known, reflected their view on the world. Reeves, however, disagreed. Their sense of humour had got her through some rather dark moments when she had first transferred from the Met. They were dependable and solid, and they always had your back, something which she was very glad of today.

'Good luck, guys.' With over thirty years in the Force under his belt, Tom Coogan was, truth to tell, glad not to be going out on a surveillance op. He was counting the days and hours now and didn't want anything to rock the boat. He was looking forward to a change of direction. Maybe he would buy that house in France after all.

'Coffee, sir?' offered Elise Palmer, who was shadowing him that month.
'Don't mind if I do.'
Elise Palmer had joined the police force later in life, after what she described as a 'portfolio career.' You name it, she'd done it – acting, secretarial work, bar work, travel agent, estate agent and masseuse. Somewhere along the line, she'd managed to fit in two boys and, once they'd grown up, a degree in Drama at Canterbury Christchurch. That got her onto an accelerated route for detective training and now, Coogan reflected with a sigh, he was lumbered with her. Trouble was, you had to mind your step around her – everyone did – because she was a protégée of Briggs. He poked at the scummy-looking froth on his cappuccino – that new coffee machine downstairs was as foul as ever - and eyed her thoughtfully. There was a lot to get on with but from what he'd seen so far, little with which she could be trusted.

Ross Norman, who seemed to be all over the place nowadays, was reporting from Radnor Park. Always sounds out of breath, Hawk thought, as, with one eye on Pippa's kitchen telly, he prepared some toast for himself and filled up Brian's water bowl. She should get that checked out. And usually spouting rubbish, anyway.
'Mr Pumpkin Head comes to Folkestone,' she announced. 'Viewers may be familiar with the character in the popular books by Dan Hawk. But, in recent weeks, the character has come, terrifyingly, to life. Police investigating the murder of John Reece, a recent graduate of the University of Kent…'
He went upstairs to get ready. As he put on his coat, he turned to look at Becky's photo.
'Be careful, darling,' she said.
'I will,' he promised. She blew him a kiss.

Downstairs, in the kitchen Ross was still burbling on. Now she was interviewing one of Reece's neighbours, an old lady. 'Such a nice young man. I've known the family for years. A

promising young actor, too.'
Actor? Hawk turned the thought over. Wasn't the other guy, Charlie Green, an actor? Resolving to check with Reeves how she was getting on with the profiling of the victims, he clicked the television off and, duffel bag slung over his shoulder, headed out. As he turned into Dyke Road, he clocked a golden brown 4 x 4, parked close in to the pavement. Most of the other car had their wheels on the pavement, and it was a tight squeeze for anyone trying to get past. No doubt there would be double yellow lines all the way down soon. Suddenly, the doors of the 4 x 4 opened, and two men emerged, one tall, one short.
'Get in, Hawk,' the shorter of the two ordered. 'We want a quick word.'
'What the…Hang on, don't I...?' With a shrug, Hawk got in, and the two men crammed in on either side of him, on the back seat. 'Well, this is cosy,' he remarked.
'I'm Detective Black.'
'And you're Detective White.' Now he remembered. Reeves had introduced them, briefly, the other evening. 'You couldn't write this shit.'
'Well, somebody did,' said Detective White, 'and you're Dan Hawk. The psychic who couldn't cut it as a cop in Folkestone and cleared off to become a writer.'
'And then swans back here as he pleases and takes on the biggest case in the last twenty years from right under our noses,' said Black.
'Look,' Hawk began. 'Briggs did say it would piss people off, but he gave me this case.'
'Want a shot of redemption after fucking off and writing these books?' asked White.
'…which may or may not be getting people killed,' added Black.
'I don't know why I am having to explain myself to you.' Hawk sighed. He was rapidly becoming tired of these two. A pair of time wasters. What was Briggs thinking, letting them out on the streets at all, and today of all days? 'But writing books was

my therapy after what happened to my wife. Ask Briggs, although I shouldn't think he wants to talk about it.'
There was silence for a moment.
'We can't let you leave, I'm afraid,' the two detectives chorused, as they pulled out pens and two copies of The Pumpkin of the Marsh. 'Without signing our books first!'
'You pair of fuckers.' Hawk shook his head.
'Had you going for a moment though,' White laughed. 'Sorry to hear about your wife and we agree, Briggs is a prick. Buckle up and we'll run you round to Marrins.'

At Marrins, preparations were also underway, inside and outside. On the face of it, everything looked normal. Bill had set out Hawk's signing table again, with some Pumpkin Head-themed fridge magnets and bookmarks – what they in the trade called publishers' swag. Punters always loved them. Reeves, Black and White were concealed in position.
Gavin Goldstein had arrived early. When Hawk had talked him through things, it had all seemed rather fun, like an episode from The Cad. Now, he wasn't so sure, and was tucking into his fourth glass of vodka, which he was pouring from a bottle under the table. As O'Neal adjusted his stab-proof collar, assuring him it was just routine, he burst out: 'Now look here, I hope this is quite safe. I've got a voiceover tomorrow.'
'I can assure you, sir,' said O'Neal, 'We are very well-prepared. Trained officers are up there on the roof tops right now.'
Clearly less than reassured, Gavin took another swig of vodka. Hawk and O'Neal exchanged glances. 'Got a right one here,' O'Neal muttered.
'Well,' Hawk said. 'Think we've got our first customer.'
Sid Hester wheeled himself into the shop and over to the table. O'Neal ducked out of the way, under an archway and into the back of the shop.
'It's Sid, isn't it?' Hawk greeted him. 'Sorry, I haven't forgotten you. I keep meaning to pop back to the pub and sign your books.'
'Well, when I heard you were doing a signing, I thought I'd

save you the trouble and I've brought them with me. First three, anyway. I need to get a copy of your latest one.'
'By the way, Sid,' Hawk said, as he began signing. 'This is Gavin Lloyd Goldstein III. You may have read that he's on board to play Mr Pumpkin Head in the movie.'
'Ah yes, indeed. The star of The Cad, no less.'
'Would you like me to do my catchphrase?' Gavin asked hopefully.
'Perhaps later,' Sid replied, 'but meanwhile could you sign my books too please?'
At the back of the shop, O'Neal's earpiece crackled. It was Reeves. 'Sir, there's a figure approaching the shop. Can't make out if it's male or female. They're all in black, carrying a large bag. They're taking something out of it. Oh shit! It's a large Pumpkin Head and they're putting it on. I'll be right down.'
Gavin signed his name in full – with a flourish – under Hawk's. 'Burt Reynolds once told me, always be nice to the public. Without them, you're nobody.' He handed the books over. 'There you are, my friend.'
'Mind if I get a selfie?' Without waiting for the reply, Sid manoeuvred himself behind the table and snapped a photo on his mobile of himself with Gavin and Hawk. Just at that moment, Mr Pumpkin Head appeared in the doorway. The figure stepped into the shop. but O'Neal had it covered. 'Hold it right there,' he said, as he appeared round the archway, gun drawn. The figure froze.
Reeves came in, Detective Black just behind her and pointed her gun at the back of its head. 'All right, everyone, stay calm. And you,' she said, 'I want you to get down on your knees and put your hands behind your back.' The figure complied, and O'Neal pulled its mask off, to reveal a woman, in her mid-thirties.
'My name is Karen Clarke,' she began, 'And I can explain everything.'
'I should hope so,' O'Neal interrupted her, 'but not here. Black, could you do the honours, please? Read her rights and take her to the station. Richard Burton – Gavin – whatever

your name is, we can let you go now.'

Gavin was about to remonstrate – and forcefully too - but he realised nobody was looking at him. A complete shower, the lot of them. Pig ignorant. He didn't include Hawk in that category of course, and, having retrieved what remained of his vodka from under the table, went to say his goodbyes. Hawk, however, was deep in conversation with the blonde policewoman who had been on the roof earlier. 'Love's young dream,' Gavin exclaimed, as he squeezed past them. He checked his watch. Time for a swift half before the train.

Sid had slipped away unnoticed in all the commotion. 'All go today, isn't it?' he muttered, under his breath as he headed towards the carpark. He wheeled himself with care past a lady who was heading for Marrins with a small stack of Dan Hawk's books. 'You're out of luck, love,' he told her. 'Signing's over for today.' He watched her trail disconsolately back across Sandgate Road. 'Hello, who's this?' he said aloud, as Gavin lurched out of the bookshop. 'A man on a mission.' He hesitated for a moment and then set off in his wake. Moments later, he watched Gavin barging into the Radnor Arms, pushing aside a young couple who were just coming out. 'Don't you know who I am?' His voice boomed, like a foghorn. Pursing his lips in disapproval, Sid turned around and wheeled away fast, in the direction from which he had come.

At the police station, Briggs clapped Hawk on the shoulder. 'Well done, Detective. Great work in apprehending the killer. Mr Pumpkin Head, or should we say Ms?'
'I'm not so sure.' Hawk shook his head. 'It seems too convenient, too neat.'
'You set the bait and she took it. Hook, line and sinker.'
'But we haven't even spoken to the suspect yet,' Hawk objected.
The telephone on Brigg's desk rang. He picked it up. 'Ah. All right. Thanks very much, Patricia. We will be down in a

minute.' He turned back to Hawk.
'That, Hawk, is something we can remedy immediately. They're ready for us in Interview Room 1. We've got our killer. I can feel it in my gut.' He slammed his fist hard into the desk as if for emphasis and immediately regretted it.
'And we all know where your gut got us last time.' Hawk thought. Deciding not to voice his thoughts, he followed Briggs downstairs and slid into a seat beside Reeves.

At the Radnor Arms, a swift half had turned into several pints for Gavin. To his delight he had found a large appreciative audience, with a chorus of Bloody Bounders! that got louder as each pint went down the hatch. A call on his mobile from his agent, checking arrangements for tomorrow's voiceover, brought him back to reality.
'Don't be late,' the girl said. 'This is a really good opportunity for you, Gavin.'
'Cheeky cow,' he thought. 'Boring too. Just when I'm having fun.' Still, she probably had a point. Bidding his new admirers goodbye, he lurched out of the pub, retracing his steps from this morning. He prided himself on a reasonable sense of direction, even if he was in his cups, rather like a homing pigeon. He spotted a man who had been on the fringes of his crowd of admirers on the other side of the road. He shouted 'Toodle pip, old chap,' but the man seemed to be in a hurry and didn't respond. Perhaps he was getting the train too. 'I'll race you,' he called.
He stopped at Tesco Express to buy some fags and a small bottle of vodka. He took a swig out of it as he staggered along, humming a few bars from Ain't Misbehavin', which had formed part of the soundtrack to The Cad.
'What the…' he protested, as he was pulled towards the stairwell of a large property.
'I am he, I am thee,' his assailant intoned. He was waving a knife around.
'Fuck right off.' Gavin had his front door keys in his pocket. He always had them ready to hand; it always helped when he

was completely rat-arsed. He slashed at his assailant with the Yale key and shoved them hard down the steps leading to the basement. There's life in the old dog yet, he thought, as he continued his unsteady progress. Nearly at the station now; he could see the park ahead. He pulled up his sleeve – his arm was bleeding. Looked like a nasty cut too. 'Fucker must have had a knife,' he said aloud. 'And hang about, what was it he said? I am he, I am thee. Christ almighty!' Feeling faint, slightly nauseous and, he had to admit it, a little frightened, he blundered on towards the bright lights of a kebab shop in search of help.

Further back towards the centre of town, a man of smallish stature almost collided with a group of revellers. He was wearing a crash helmet and seemed to be cradling his hand. 'You all right, mate?' they called to him, but he walked off. 'Ooh, a man on a mission,' they called. 'Where's your motorbike then?'

Karen Clarke sat nervously in Interview Room 1, a plastic cup of water untouched in front of her. She explained that she worked for an agency. 'They work with authors and they do book launches and publicity too, that sort of thing. And last night, they rang me to say they wanted somebody dressed in black robes and a pumpkin mask to help with a book launch.'

'For fuck's sake! Did they not give a name?' Elise Palmer burst out, anxious to make an impression. Truth be told, she had been finding this work-shadowing a bit tedious. Plod work, she called it.

Detective Coogan slapped her down with a furious glare. 'You are only supposed to be observing.'

'I can give you the name,' said Karen. 'Vic Barkworth? Barkley? Phone the agency if you don't believe me. They're in London, near Leicester Square.'

'That won't be necessary, Ms Clarke. Interview terminated at 16.30 hours.' Hawk pushed his chair back.

'What the hell are you doing, Hawk?' Briggs was beginning to wonder whether he had made a serious mistake in taking Hawk (and the psychic crap that went with him) back on.

Unorthodox methods were dangerous, he'd been told, all those years ago. Mavericks like Hawk were even more so.
'Vic Barkley,' Hawk explained, in that infuriating manner of his, 'is my fucking literary agent. How's your gut now, Superintendent Briggs?'
'I am sorry, Ms. Clarke,' Hawk continued, 'Somebody will drive you home. Jesus Christ.'
He stormed out of the interview room. Coogan pushed a set of car keys over to Palmer. 'There you go. A proper assignment for you. You keep saying you want one.'
'What, all the way back to London?' Palmer was aghast. 'I've got plans tonight. My dance class…'
'Orpington, actually,' Karen put in. 'If that helps. But I don't want to be any trouble. I'd better just ring my solicitor on the way and tell him I'm being released.'
O'Neal, who had also been observing, shook his head as he watched the ladies go off together. Palmer was a fast driver. He hoped her passenger had a strong stomach. He turned to Reeves. 'Been a few developments. Well, that's an understatement. Meet you round at Hawk's in an hour?'
'Copy that,' Reeves replied.

Outside the police station, Treva Parkinson, reporter with the Kent Bugle had been waiting patiently. His boss had been lambasting him in recent months about the fact that they never got a scoop, threatened him with being out of a job. Well, it looked as if he might be lucky this time. A telephone call from a friend who'd been heading down to Marrins for the book signing, seen the commotion and put two and two together. And – bingo – here was Dan Hawk coming out. He stepped forward.
'Dan Hawk?' he began. 'I'm Treva Parkinson from the Kent Bugle. Is it true that you have apprehended the so-called Mr Pumpkin Head killer?'
Hawk didn't break his stride. 'A false alarm, I'm afraid.'
'They're still out there then?'
'Somewhere,' Hawk replied. 'Look, I can't discuss the case any

further at this point. But what I can say is that I intend to nail the son-of-a bitch one way or another.'
Treva watched as Hawk disappeared around the corner. An exclusive; perhaps not the news everyone wanted, but an exclusive all the same.

Coogan sat on a bench along the Leas. Although it was autumn, it was a balmy night and quite pleasant. Nobody was about tonight though. He listened with half an ear to the inane banter between Gavin Goldstein and his colleague, Detective Fisher. Drafted in to help with the inquiry, Fisher, from what Coogan could discern, was a lifelong fan of Gavin's. It had been quite an evening. A call from the hospital to say that they had Goldstein, that he had been in some sort of affray and that he was ready to be discharged and could somebody please come and get him? A bit of entertaining to and fro-ing, after they'd taken a statement, with Goldstein vacillating between checking in at The View, which was why they were out here, and heading home, as he did have a voiceover to get to the next day and timing was a bit tight. The killer was still out there, and they were organising an escort to get Goldstein back to Hampstead. It was going to be Coogan as far as Saint Pancras and then they'd hand him over to a Met officer – PC Sam Dinnage - for the final leg.
'That's Dinnage with two ns? And hold on - just the one officer for the escort? Are you sure? I should have thought…Oh, I see. Well, that's understandable.' Coogan turned to Fisher. 'Right. All arranged. Just the one officer; there was a big demo in central London earlier, with a few arrests. It's been all hands to the pump for them. Anyway, we're meeting him on the concourse as you go into the underground.'
'I think Gavin is too far gone to go on the train,' Detective Fisher observed. 'And the View just rang to say they're full anyway. Seems a bit odd on a school night, but there you go. We'll have to wait until he sobers up. That could be a while and I'm still meant to be on duty. Although I honestly don't

mind…'

'Oh, sod that,' Coogan replied. 'Let's give him half an hour then. It could take me at least that long to get a car organised, unless…' He dialled Palmer's number on his mobile.

'Coogan here. Where are you?' he asked.

'Coming in towards Ashford,' she replied. 'Traffic has been fine. Nice lady.'

'I need a favour,' Coogan began. 'Got to escort our actor friend up to London and hand him over to the Met at Saint Pancras. Slight change of plan. We need a driver.' Glancing behind him, he noticed a man walking briskly across the grass. The fellow seemed to have come out of the shadows, out of nowhere. Strange. Oh well. He hoped the man hadn't been listening in. Perhaps he had been rather careless. Still, what would anyone eavesdropping have made of it all? He watched the man disappear down one of the side roads and turned his attention back to Palmer 'About half an hour then? You're a star.'

He left Fisher and Goldstein to their chat (he was giving her his autograph now, for God's sake) and closed his eyes. It had been an incredibly long day and it looked as if it was going to be an equally long night. How long was it until his retirement now? Two hundred and eighty- four days and how many night shifts? It was like counting sheep. He started to drift off.

'Your lift's here.' Detective Fisher nudged him awake. 'And I had better be getting back to work,' It's been great meeting you, Gavin.'

'Likewise,' replied Gavin. 'Bye, Sharon.'

'It's Stacey,' she corrected him. 'I know, you wouldn't believe it, would you?'

'Give me strength,' Coogan groaned. 'See you back at the station soon.' He turned to Goldstein. 'Our lift is here. Detective Palmer will drive us to Saint Pancras and then we're handing you over to a Met officer for the last stage of the journey.'

'Awfully decent of you, old chap,' Gavin replied, as he lumbered over towards the railings. 'Better siphon the python

first.'
'God almighty.' Coogan got into the front seat beside Palmer. 'You're always saying you want to do some proper police work. Been quite a day so far.'
Palmer agreed. She enjoyed driving, despite Coogan's teasing, and it certainly beat being at the station, going through paperwork. Her lack of attention to detail was becoming increasingly apparent. People were beginning to comment on it. Today, however, had been fun. She and Karen Clarke had got on like a house on fire.

Back at Pippa's, Hawk, Reeves and O'Neal were assembled in the living room.
'Well, where do we start?' O'Neal sipped thoughtfully at a beer. 'Have a look at this. It was found at John Reece's. Looks as if he might have tried to use it as a weapon. Have a look at page eight.'
Reeves handed Hawk a magazine in a sealed plastic cover. Inside, was a magazine – Acting Up Weekly, an industry magazine for the acting profession. On its cover was a large photograph of Gavin Lloyd Goldstein. Reece had circled the 'In Memoriam' section and the names Charlie Green, Beverley Katharine Smithe and John Carlton-Jones.
Hawk got up to refill his glass. 'So, it's official. Reece was an actor too?'
'He was,' O'Neal replied. 'And there's more. Reeves here has been doing some sterling work. It seems all the victims had been given a part in a new play that's going to open in the West End, by a director named Jed Cabot. Reece had just been cast too. Oh, and forensics came back about that piece of metal stuck into his forehead. It had some writing on it. 'Most Promising,' it says. Probably an ornament or statue.'
'What about Goldstein?' Hawk asked. He had a bad feeling. All right, the guy was as irritating as hell, and God alone knew why someone had seen fit to cast him in the film, but he must be a prime target now, surely. He wasn't surprised when O'Neal told him that Mr Pumpkin Head had attacked Goldstein on the

way to Folkestone Central; jumped out on him from a stairwell and slashed at him with a knife. Goldstein still had his stab proof collar on and managed to fend him off. He cut Mr Pumpkin Head on the hand with a key and gave him a shove and was very proud about that.

'He got a nasty cut on his arm in return, but they've checked him over at the hospital and now he's going up to London, with a police escort,' O'Neal explained.

'No CCTV then? Or passers-by?' It was incredible, Hawk thought, how Mr Pumpkin Head seemed to be able to pop up everywhere, unseen, just like in the books.

'He always chooses places without much coverage,' O'Neal replied, 'and nobody's reported anything. Not yet, anyway.'

'Perhaps he is in disguise before the attacks. And afterwards,' Hawk suggested.

'I will double check CCTV and whether anyone caught anything on their doorbells,' Reeves offered.

O'Neal headed off back to the station. Coogan was a safe pair of hands, he assured Hawk. 'He hasn't changed since your time. Doesn't rock the boat, and he's winding the clock down to retirement, but he'll make sure Goldstein gets home safely.'

Hawk, however, was miles away, wondering whether they might just have narrowed Mr Pumpkin Head's identity down to a disgruntled, overlooked actor. Reeves cleared her throat. He looked at her, as if surprised that she was still there.

'Mind if I ask you something?'

'Fire away,' Hawk replied.

'Your wife,' she began. 'What does she make of all this?'

'My gift?'

'Yes.'

'I often talk to her about it.'

'Are you sure you're not just talking to the trees?'

'I thought you said you weren't all dicks down here,' Hawk retorted.

Reeves got up. 'I'd better be off,' she said, but Hawk didn't acknowledge her. As she walked down the steps to her car, she cursed her big mouth. Every sodding time, honestly. She really was a walking disaster area, when it came to relationships, friendships even.

Hawk went upstairs to fetch his coat. When he got one of his hunches, like now, he just had to act on it. 'Where are you?' he asked Becky. 'I need to talk to you. You do know there will never be anyone else, don't you?' Becky just looked out of the frame at him with an enigmatic smile. Was he seeing things - he seemed to be doing an awful lot of this lately – or did she shake her head, very slightly? 'I've got to go, Becky. See you later love.' Downstairs, he took a slug of whisky and then opened the front door. Brian shot out in front of him, almost tripping him up. 'We're both on the prowl tonight, mate,' Hawk said. 'Don't do anything I wouldn't.'

7 CAD

In the car park at Pleydell Gardens, Sid got into the front seat of his blue Peugeot. Specially adapted for him, it was his pride and joy. He glanced in the mirror – there was nobody about. With his disabled sticker, he could park anywhere, but he liked this car park, especially at night. He got into the front seat and turned the radio on, flicking through the channels in search of a play, something to entertain him, but all that was coming over the airwaves tonight was a load of vacuous chatter. He got quite enough of that at the Hut. He switched it off again and sat in silence, the engine ticking over. It was cold now and very dark. He hadn't intended staying out so late. Fred was manning the fort at the pub and had just texted to say there was nothing much doing and that he might close soon. He tossed a coin twice. It didn't help. He watched the numbers on the clock tick round to the hour. There was still time. He picked up his mobile.

'Gustav, mate,' he began. 'You know that favour you owe me. It's one hell of a long shot, but…where are you right now? You are? You could? Is she really? Well now, that's marvellous. Yes, we must meet up for a pint soon. Why don't you come down again and visit?' He inched the car forward and turned towards town. The large suitcase in the back slid around every time he braked. He would have to do something about that. It was bloody annoying.

PC Sam Dinnage had arrived in good time at Kings Cross, for his escort duty. He stood on the concourse, at the meeting point. He had to pinch himself sometimes, as a young man from a small town in the Derbyshire Dales, to make sure that he wasn't dreaming and that he was here, in the middle of London, and on his very first 'solo' assignment. With Gavin Goldstein from The Cad, no less. His parents loved that show.

His attention was caught by a couple having an argument. Nothing unusual at this time of night and they'd probably had a few drinks. They looked rather mismatched. She was tall and blonde, probably this side of thirty. In a smart navy overcoat, she looked like a City worker. The man was considerably older, in a suit that strained over his paunch, hair obviously dyed, grizzled-looking.

'I'll fucking knock you into next week,' the man shouted, almost dragging his partner towards the escalator.

'Let go of me!' she protested.

PC Dinnage looked at his watch. He was still a little early and they would probably be ages yet, coming up from Kent, enough time to break this up. A few well-chosen words would do, as he'd been taught during his training. He set off after the pair.

'We're here,' Palmer announced. She pulled up outside the entrance to the Eurostar terminal. Both her passengers had been snoring in unison since Maidstone. They had made excellent time. She knew how to get her foot down. Those years of London driving - you never forgot - stood her in great stead. 'Where are you meeting Mr Goldstein's escort again?'

Coogan rubbed his eyes. 'Oh, on the other side, by the underground sign on the concourse, but the walk will do me good.' He got out, wincing slightly, yawned and stretched and opened the door to the back seat. 'Let's be having you, then mate.'

'I'll tuck myself in somewhere and then I know this place in Soho that stays open late, near Ronnie Scott's. Does fabulous coffee and a mean tiramisu,' Palmer suggested. 'Come on. I've been driving nonstop for hours. I'm parched.'

'All right.' A cup of coffee- whether fabulous or not, sounded just the ticket. 'See you in a minute then. Let's see if our chap has arrived.'

Coogan and Goldstein walked through the station. 'Still can't Adam and Eve it,' Goldstein was holding forth. 'The role I was born to play, and then this fucker comes out of nowhere and starts slashing at me. You wait till I…'

'Keep your voice down,' Coogan advised. 'You're not out of

danger yet. Is Mr Barkley sending a car for you tomorrow? Might be an idea.'
'No, I'll just get an Uber tomorrow, they're very good,' Goldstein replied. 'This voiceover - it's an advertisement for a drinks company – some twenties-themed thing. I hope I'll get some freebies. I'm in a lot of demand you know.'
It was getting late and most of the commuters had gone, as had the last Eurostar. A group who had clearly been for after-work drinks were saying their goodbyes, checking their mobiles and heading their separate ways. They didn't recognise Goldstein; most of them, Coogan noted with amusement, would have been toddlers when The Cad had been on. That clearly irked his companion. Goldstein continued with his monologue on all the new opportunities coming his way. As they approached the concourse, Coogan spotted a Metropolitan police officer. The man was a similar age to him, medium height, brown hair, going a bit grey. He smiled as they approached.
'Detective Sergeant Coogan?' the officer said, flashing a warrant card at bewildering speed. 'I'm PC Dinnage. Sam Dinnage.' Coogan noticed that the man was wearing smart black leather gloves and wondered whether they were standard issue for the Met; it wasn't that cold yet, surely. Still, they were rather nice, and it was a relief to be handing his charge over to an experienced officer.
Coogan clapped Goldstein on the shoulder. 'Well, I am leaving you in this gentleman's capable hands. Look after yourself now.' With that, he made his way back to Palmer's car, and got in. 'All done. Soho, Jeeves, and don't spare the horses.' Palmer drove skilfully through the back doubles into the West End, and they were soon tucking into a bowl of tiramisu each, washed down with a cortado ('Try it, it's nice,' Palmer urged,) perched on stools at the long zinc counter.

Hawk, in the meantime, had been on a trajectory of Folkestone's finest drinking establishments. He glanced at his watch. Time for another, for the road. His mood was bleak.

Becky seemed to be withdrawing from him. Drawing a complete blank on this case was troubling him. That bastard – his own creation – was still out there. He had hoped the book signing would have flushed him out, but only one person had turned up – his number one fan, Sid. There was something strangely familiar and at the same time odd about that fellow and, come to think of it, his voice. 'Something of the night.' He tried to recall who had coined that phrase as he turned into Cheriton Place, making for the Firkin Ale House. He was glad to see it still going strong; it had been a favourite haunt of his and Becky's. He stood at the bar, perusing a long list of beers and ciders and trying to decipher the names on the barrels. He gave up. You couldn't go wrong here.

'What can I do for you?' the landlord asked.

'Pint of the top righthand one please.' As it was poured for him, Hawk became aware of another customer standing beside him. With his unkempt hair and eye patch, the man put him in mind of a character from a children's series he had watched on television, many years ago. The man was clearly itching to strike up a conversation and he did.

'Sorry for intruding, but you're that writer chap, aren't you? I love your books, man.'

'Thank you.' Hawk paid for his pint and took it upstairs, hoping that the man who, he had noticed, walked with a stick, would not follow him. However, he did, and hovered beside the table where Dan had sat down. Relenting, Hawk motioned for him to join him. Perhaps some company would do him good. Becky was always telling him he should make more of an effort.

The man introduced himself. 'Dwight Roberts.' He cleared his throat. 'You must feel like shit, seeing that somebody has taken on your creation and is killing people for real.'

'You've no idea,' Hawk replied. 'What happened to your eye?'

'I'm a Falklands veteran.'

'Sorry to hear that.'

'I'm not bitter,' Dwight explained. 'We veterans, we've just been fighting a rich man's war, doing the government's dirty

work.'
'Are you a member of Veterans for Peace by any chance?'
'You bet.' Dwight took a sip of his drink. 'A conflict is usually about land or stealing minerals or brainwashing people with our religion. Blow the fucking place up and then get some lucrative deals rebuilding it. Usual crap.'
Hawk raised his glass in a toast. That, although laden with cynicism, wasn't a bad summary at all. A young cousin of Becky's had been killed in Afghanistan, a few years ago. Nineteen years old. He still felt angry when he watched the news. Nothing had been learned. He looked across at Dwight. 'Have you ever come across the landlord at the Shepherd's Hut, out on the Marsh? I think his name is Sidney Hester.'
'Sid Hester? Or should I say Cid – with a C – Heston?' A look of distaste came over Dwight's face. 'I haven't been out there in ages. Let's just say I had a falling out with him. He told me he was in the Falklands conflict, but I didn't believe him. Said he was in 'classified ops.' Always a dead giveaway. If you ask me, he's just a puffed-up old fraud.'
'All the same, 'Hawk observed. 'It can't be easy for him, running a pub. He's been there for a while, hasn't he? Got to admire the guy's tenacity.'
Dwight snorted. 'Wouldn't be surprised if he was putting that on too. Take a good look at him next time and you'll see what I mean. Anyway, as I told you, he's full of bullshit.'
Hawk took a tenner out of his pocket and put it on the table in front of Dwight. 'I must go,' he said, 'but it has been good to talk to you. Have a couple of pints on me.'
'Very kind of you, sir' Dwight replied. 'As Johnny Cash once said, I might be AGAINST the wars, but I am FOR the warriors.'

At the police station, Reeves was going through CCTV images on a computer. O'Neal drew a chair up next to her and sat down. 'Any joy?' he asked.
'Not really. Not yet. There's no clear footage – at least as far as I can make out – of Mr Pumpkin Head.' She brought up a

grainy still. 'This is just before Reece was attacked. Can you see – I think it's a lady in a headscarf? Nobody else about.'

She pulled up the next image. 'This evening, just before Goldstein was attacked, I reckon that's a guy wearing a crash helmet, but he was in the next road, that runs parallel. And outside the Radnor – I think this guy is wearing a ski mask. Strange. Nothing of course on Charlie Green; that was right out in the sticks.'

'I went through some footage from Peterborough,' said O'Neal. 'CCTV wasn't working in the area where Beverley was, but the camera did catch a chap with long straggly hair and a scruffy beard, which bears out the evidence from the lady in the gift shop. And then remember the Met sent us the image of the guy in the street behind the London dungeon, with the baseball cap? There must be…'

Reeves went back to the first image. 'You know,' she commented, 'Hawk wondered from the outset whether the killer could be in disguise, before he puts on his Mr Pumpkin Head garb, and perhaps afterwards too. Do you notice something about all these images, something they have in common?'

O'Neal peered at the screen. 'Can't say I do.'

'Well, it may be something and nothing,' she continued, 'but they're all wearing a black rucksack. The lady in the headscarf, the guy behind the London Dungeon and this person with the crash helmet. Looks like the same rucksack to me.'

They glanced at each other. Could this be the breakthrough they were hoping for?

'It's got to be more than a coincidence. We'll catch up with Hawk tomorrow morning,' said Reeves. 'And see how he's been getting on.'

Gavin Goldstein and his escort alighted from the tube at Hampstead and made their way up to the surface in the high-speed lift. 'Deepest platforms on the network,' Gavin told his companion. 'Built on a steep hill, you see. Seventeen storeys below the surface. There are steps but I wouldn't fancy them

right now.' Gavin could – and frequently did – bore for Europe on the subject. There was nobody else about now to hear his lecture; it was that lull between the late-night shoppers and after-work tipplers and the theatre goers.
'A nightcap at the Flask?' Goldstein enquired, more in hope than in expectation. 'Should be able to get one in just before last orders, if we look slippy?'
'Better not, sir. I'm still on duty. Though it's a nice pub, isn't it? A while since I was last there.'
They chatted amicably as Goldstein led the way into a quiet cul-de-sac. He stopped outside a small Arts and Crafts property. He had inherited it from his Aunt Hettie and, as the royalties had dried up over the years, he had neglected it somewhat. It had been quite some time since the lightbulbs had been replaced in the colourful Tiffany lanterns which used to illuminate the garden. As a child, he had loved them and the light they cast. Now, they both needed repairing, and, he had to admit, the house looked scruffy and unloved. Hopefully, that was all about to change.
'This is me,' he said. The gate creaked on its hinges as he pushed it open and walked up the black and white tiled path. 'Mind how you go. It can be a little treacherous at this time of year, with the leaves. You just can't get the help nowadays.' He reached into his pocket for his keys. 'Thank you so much for escorting me, Officer.'
'That's quite all right, sir. It's all part of the service.'
'I can't help thinking,' Goldstein said, 'that I've met you before somewhere, although I can't think where.'
'I don't recall, sir, although we policemen do tend to look alike.'
'I must be mistaken then.'
The policeman cleared his throat. 'I wonder, sir, I do hope it isn't too much of an imposition, but before I go, would you mind saying your catchphrase for me? The thing is, my wife and I loved you in The Cad and it would be great if I could record it on my phone. I don't want to keep you though.'
'Of course. Here we go then. Are you ready? Bloody

Bounders!' Now, he hoped, the tedious little oik would bugger off. It had been a long day and he was in need of a glass of whisky before turning in. 'Thanks again. Goodnight,' he called, and, hoping it was a strong enough hint, turned around to unlock his door. Like everything else in Aunt Hettie's house, as he still thought of it, the door needed some attention and it took some force to open it. He fumbled for the light switch and then remembered that the chandelier had finally gone off to be repaired. It had been badly damaged some months ago, at a wild party of which he had only a vague memory. He'd stopped holding them after that.

'I've got one for you now, sir.' The voice came from right behind him.

'Oh, what's that?' Goldstein's patience was wearing rather thin now. He was desperate for a pee. He had a good mind to shoo the man out and close the door, but then again, he did seem to be a genuine fan and now he had been cast in the role he was born to play, it wouldn't do to be rude all the time. He was going to have to curb his instincts. He turned around. The policeman's head was now covered by a large papier mâché pumpkin. He had removed his gloves, and Goldstein could see the gash on the man's hand. 'Oh shit!' he exclaimed. 'I am he, I am thee,' the policeman recited as he lunged forwards.

Some moments later, his handiwork complete, the policeman rose from Goldstein's lifeless body. The light from the bronze Art Deco lamp on the occasional table was dim but adequate for his purposes. He wondered whether to close those unseeing eyes. Not doing so seemed faintly disrespectful, but he had several other matters to attend to instead. He took off his uniform, folded it neatly and put it in the rucksack. He changed into a pair of black slacks and a black polo neck jumper. He picked up the pumpkin head, examined it carefully and put it in the rucksack too.

He set off on a tour around the house. Just the type of gaff he would have expected, although the idle sod had clearly not looked after it. He paused by a mahogany cabinet of ivory netsuke and gave a low whistle. Must be worth a mint. Poised to scoop them all into his rucksack, he hesitated. Maybe better not; selling this lot would be a challenge and even if they weren't insured up to the hilt, their provenance would be well known to any collectors worth their salt. A moment later, he slipped a small carved camel into his pocket. He began closing all the curtains. Somehow, it seemed fitting.

He nearly jumped out of his skin upstairs, when he came across a black Crombie. On the outside of the wardrobe, it looked for all the world as if somebody was hanging there. The room seemed not to have been used for a long time. It smelt faintly of mothballs. On an impulse, he slipped the coat off its hanger. It had clearly been made for someone of a smaller stature than Goldstein. It fitted him well. He picked up a black Fedora from the tallboy, put it on and admired himself in the mirror. 'These will do nicely,' he murmured and walked down the stairs and past the body, picking up the rucksack on the way. He pocketed the keys which Goldstein had dropped on the floor and, with a jaunty 'Cheerio, old chap,' pulled the door firmly to and walked down the path. He turned into the High street, wondering whether there was time to visit the graveyard at Saint John's. It had been a while since he had visited Captain Hook's grave. He passed an elderly lady being taken for a walk by a dachshund and raised his Fedora to her politely. The dog growled at him. 'Charmed, I'm sure,' he muttered. He checked his watch. It was later than he thought, so he headed straight for the Tube station.

PC Sam Dinnage had waited dutifully at Euston for a good couple of hours, having first broken up the fight between the odd couple. His immediate superior, after one hell of an evening at the station – knifings, theft, sexual assault, you name it – had seemed rather distracted but had agreed that Sam should hang on for a while longer. 'Traffic can be bad up from – where are they coming from – Margate?' He had telephoned again and been told that his boss was just going off duty but would ring the Kent police station in the morning and give them a piece of his mind, although, as he would soon learn, sometimes plans just changed at a moment's notice. He headed down onto the Northern line, on a long escalator. Coming up on the other side was a man in a black overcoat and Fedora hat. Could almost have been his grandfather, he thought, as his tube pulled in. That was how he used to dress.

Hawk walked unsteadily up the hill towards Pippa's. 'Hello, what's this?' A white Astra was parked neatly outside. He patted the bonnet. 'You'll do,' he murmured. A set of keys had been posted through the door in an envelope with a piece of paper that simply said: 'Sorry.'

With a mug of tea at his side, Hawk pulled up the Falklands War Records. He typed in Sidney Hester, trying different spellings just in case. Then he tried the name Dwight had given him. Cidney Heston. Was it a nickname perhaps? Dwight had been quite emphatic that it was Cidney with a C. He tried it with a 'y' again – Cyd – and then typed 'Cid Heston' into a different search engine one more time. Nothing came up, apart from a clip from El Cid with Charlton Heston. 'Bugger it,' he muttered. 'I'm going to bed.'

O'Neal was on his way home. He'd had a call, just before he left, from a detective in Peterborough. They'd been to see a sculptress in a nearby village, Wansford. She had telephoned the station when she had heard the news about Mr Pumpkin Head. She had been commissioned to carve the small pumpkin which had appeared in the cathedral and which had only been noticed just after Beverley Katharine Smithe's murder.

'I thought it was odd,' she'd told them. 'Ever such a rushed job. I struggled to finish it in time.'

'Did she ever see anything of her client?' O'Neal had asked. Not specifically, came the reply. The finished article had been left, in accordance with instructions, outside her home, which was down a narrow country lane, and then the fee had been left in cash in a box just inside the gate. However, she had looked out of the upstairs window on a whim and seen a blue car pulling away fast. She had not, unfortunately, caught sight of the number plate and, as she 'didn't know much about cars,' could not say what make it was. It may have been a Renault, or maybe a Peugeot. Sometimes, people stopped at the house next door to buy eggs, so she couldn't be one hundred percent sure that this was her customer. She had given the police permission to access her telephone records. There had been a few calls which turned out to be from telephone boxes in different locations across the Fens. That was rather odd.

'A blue Peugeot, or possibly a Renault. That covers a multitude of sins,' O'Neal sighed, as he pulled up outside his house, in the Golden Valley, which, since his long-term girlfriend had moved away, seemed very quiet. He knew Wansford; his grandparents had lived there. He remembered trips to the Haycock Hotel and his granny telling him why the place was called 'Wansford-in-England,' although for the life of him, he couldn't remember the reason now. Anyway, they were no closer to finding this bastard and Briggs was going to be asking questions soon. He let himself in and put the kettle on, and then picked up his mobile and dialled Reeves's number. She answered straightaway.

'Can you make it in a little earlier tomorrow? I'm a bit concerned about this bloody Pumpkin Head.'

'See you bright and early at seven. I'll pick you up, if you like?' came the reply.

In West Hythe, Thaddeus Moncrieff switched off the wireless. More about this monster with a pumpkin for a head – a head which, almost certainly, he had fashioned and then, to add insult to injury, painted. He was sick of hearing about it. Come to think of it, how had this person found him? He didn't exactly advertise his services nowadays, although any extra cash was always welcome. Anyway, one thing was for certain, he was buggered if he was going to put himself out there by telephoning the police. What could he tell them, anyway? He did have telephone numbers of course. He'd dialled 1471 after each of the mysterious calls and got different numbers each time. Some local, some London. He had written them all down in his notebook, as a precaution.

He hadn't solved the mystery of the missing painting. The gallery in Rye did not have it. Why on earth though would somebody wish to steal a watercolour of Gratitude Farm? It wasn't even one of his best, although he'd liked its symmetry with the rest of his collection. He went over to the front door and checked that it was locked and bolted. He stirred up the fire and watched in satisfaction as it blazed up.

8 CLUES

Upstairs at Pippa's, Brian was perched, sphinx-like, at the end of Hawk's bed. This seemed to be his regular sleeping spot now; he had abandoned his basket downstairs. Hawk had tried to shoo him off a few times, unsure as to whether the cat was even meant to be upstairs. He had a feeling that this was not the case. Brian, however, always reappeared. Now, Hawk was in a troubled sleep, in and out of dreams. Images came and went, as if he was in a cinema. First, the crowd from the police station; Briggs saying: 'I'm giving you the chance to right the wrongs' and White asking if he wanted a shot at redemption. Reeves appeared then. 'Can I suggest you write a book about kittens next time?' Dwight Roberts shuffled into view. 'He told me he was in the Falklands conflict, but I just didn't believe him.' Reeves came back with: 'I'm sure some actors would quite literally kill for the part.' Goldstein chipped in next, with 'Bloody Bounders,' and then O'Neal with: 'It appears to have writing on it. Most promising, it says.' Then he heard his own voice. 'Disgruntled actor.' A figure in a black overcoat and Fedora flickered past very quickly. He heard his own voice again: 'What the actual…?'

The next image was the cover of Rousing Hereward. Hawk had been particularly pleased with that cover. With the earlier books, he'd let Vic and the publisher get on with it, but this time he'd stayed with his sister in Peterborough for the night. Her husband was a keen member of a local historical re-enactment society, and they went out with a photographer at sunrise, capturing the wide, arable Fenlands fields and Hereward's army in the distance. You could just make Mr Pumpkin Head out in the corner of the picture. Then, in his dream a long knife was plunged into the cover. Finally, Hawk's laptop appeared, with the words 'El Cid Heston.'

Hawk woke up at this and sat bolt upright. Brian's fur was standing on end, as if he were a cartoon cat. He jumped off the bed and went and sat in the arm chair, studiously licking a paw.

Becky waved at Hawk from the photo frame. 'I thought perhaps you could do with a little help,' she said. Hawk blew her a kiss and leapt out of bed. He pulled on some clothes, went downstairs and settled back down in front of the computer screen.

A newspaper search quickly brought up a story in the South London Sentinel, from the early noughties, and a large picture with the caption 'Most promising actor Cidney Heston in Freak Accident.' That was Sid Hester all right, holding a large trophy aloft.

Sipping at a coffee, Hawk scrolled through the article. Cid Heston had won his award after playing the leading role in a production of Pudding Hill, an experimental new play. On the strength of this, he was given another leading role, this time in a play by young up and coming playwright Jed Capot, which was to be staged at the Dingwall, a theatre based in an old warehouse in East Croydon. Cid hadn't performed there before, and the place had its quirks. Exasperated by a stream of comments from Malory Goodman, the stage director, one afternoon, to the effect that she couldn't see him from where she was and his positioning must be incorrect, he had shouted: 'Are you blind as well as incredibly dense, you ridiculous woman?' The next moment, he had grabbed one of the stage lights, thinking to brandish it over himself, with a 'Now can you see me?' Unfortunately, he was electrocuted. The article went on to say that Cid had received severe burns and, reacting to the shock, had jumped backwards off the stage, causing devastating spinal injuries.

There was no further press coverage on Cid. Scrolling on, Hawk noted that Malory Goodman had died two years ago, having fallen off the cliff at St Margaret's Bay. The coroner had found nothing untoward although her family had commented that she was the last person to have suicidal tendencies and that she was an experienced hiker who would surely have known not to stray close to the edge. Jed Capot was, of course, well-known. Hawk had taken Becky to see one of his plays once. In fact, hadn't they recently been casting for one of his

new plays, Slaybrook, with several of Mr Pumpkin Head's victims already in it? He made a note on Reeves's board and then dialled her number.
'Must be telepathy,' she said. 'We're just on our way to you. We've got coffee and bacon sarnies from Buttys. And doughnuts too. How's it going?'
'All good.'
'By the way,' O'Neal took a swig of coffee. 'DC Reeves has been going through the CCTV and you're right – Mr Pumpkin Head may have been in disguise before he put his gear on. And perhaps afterwards too.'
'Good work,' Hawk replied, 'but I can do you one better. I think I know who the killer is. I've just got to check a theory out. Now listen, both of you. This is my mess and I have got to sort it out on my own. I don't want either of you, or anybody else for that matter, to get hurt.'
He hung up. O'Neal looked at Reeves.
'I don't think…' he began. Reeves shook her head, executed a neat U turn and they drove in silence back to the police station.

Hawk dashed upstairs. He reckoned – he wasn't sure why – that he had a window of an hour. There was no time to lose. He taped a pocketknife to his shin, grabbed his car keys and made his way to the door. He turned around when he heard Becky's voice. 'Take me with you,' she said. He slid her photograph carefully out of the frame and put it in his pocket.
He pulled up outside a building in Cheriton and dashed inside. He tapped in an access code – it still worked. Good. He walked along a corridor, into his lock-up, and looked around. All Becky's things that he couldn't bear to part with and some of his own, all present and correct. A set of golf clubs and, in the corner, there was a small airport holdall. He unzipped it. Inside was a Magnum 44. After Becky's death, wondering what vipers' nest his West London enquiries might have stirred up, and whether he would be next on the list, he had acquired it, via the murky channels of the local underworld. Clint Eastwood's gun in Dirty Harry, one of his favourite movies;

somehow that seemed fitting. He'd left it behind when he moved away.
'Well,' he murmured. 'It's been a long time.'

Shouldering the holdall, he hurried back out to the car, giving a friendly wave to the bored youth on the reception desk, and pulled into a line of traffic. Through Shorncliffe and down the hill into Hythe; he had to stop just before the Light Railway Station, to allow a convoy of vehicles onto the field nearby. Zoom Events, the sign said. They must be setting up for the Autumn Festival. Just before he lost Becky, they'd been to one of those, and in some unseasonably fine weather, had spent the afternoon wandering round the food stalls and listening to the bands, singing along to Dumb Little Country Boy. They'd even stumbled across a cookery display by two complete lunatics called The King Elvises.
Only the other night though, Becky had told him he needed to start going out again.
'I can't, Becks.'
'You must, Dan.' And with that, with a sound like a crackly transistor, he'd lost contact with her. Not permanently, thank goodness, although every time, it seemed to be getting more difficult. Unless he was imagining things. He felt the photograph buzz in his pocket as he drove and breathed a sigh of relief.

In Hampstead, commuters were hurrying past Gavin Goldstein's house. A knot of schoolchildren jostled each other on the pavement. Dora Adler, a neighbour, on her way to the park with her little dachshund, glanced across the road and tutted at the state of it. Dear Hettie would be rotating in her grave. The dachshund, whose name was Mitzi, gave an irritable bark, as if in support. Inside Gavin's house, the telephone rang, and Vic Barkley's voice echoed in the hall. 'Tried you on your mobile and it seems to be switched off. Anyway, I hope everything is all right at your end; I was wondering why you didn't turn up at the voiceover this morning. Ring me as soon as you get this. Ciao, ciao!'

Vic unscrewed the lid of his fountain pen – a good one, which he had been given for his fiftieth. He reached for a new bottle of ink. The contract had just come through for the Mr Pumpkin Head film, the first of several. He fervently hoped Goldstein would not, as Hawk had predicted, be a nightmare and ruin it for them all. He had not appreciated one little bit the young whippersnapper from the ad company who had chewed his ear off earlier, as if he were Goldstein's keeper. On an impulse, he flipped through his Rolodex – he had never really got to grips with computers – and found the number of Goldstein's agent, Zelda Buchanan. He couldn't help thinking it was rather a pretentious name and, he would wager, not the one she was born with.

'Oh, he's terrible with phone calls,' Zelda chirped. 'Forgets to take his mobile with him or has it on silent, or so he says. He does have a habit now of going into Hampstead High Street in the morning for a coffee and croissant and reading the newspapers. I will check up on him though. I find just before lunch is a good time to get him. Laters!'

'Laters indeed,' Vic thought. He glanced at his watch. Zelda's mention of coffee and croissants had made him hungry. He locked the office and headed down the stairs to his favourite place in Wardour Street. As he nibbled at a pain au chocolat, he couldn't help feeling uneasy about Goldstein and rang Hawk's number, but there was no response. 'Not you as well,' he murmured. 'And if nobody else can be arsed, I'll just have to go over there myself. I'll take the contract with me and get him to sign it.'

As he made his way through the crowds at Leicester Square, he wondered whether Hawk had been right after all. Securing Goldstein had seemed such a coup. Now, he was turning out to be a nightmare. He began to think about alternatives. Treva Etienne would, if available, be a popular choice. Kirsty Cox owed him a favour or two and she really would be great. Then, if he could possibly be prevailed upon, there was Geoffrey

Deuel.
'Goldstein, you fool, you're in the last chance saloon,' he murmured, as he hopped onto a north-bound tube.

At the police station, Coogan rushed up to Brigg's office, coffee in hand. Now what, he wondered? By the time he and Palmer had got back from London it had been nearly three o'clock; just enough time for some shut-eye. Briggs' tone was icy.
'Perhaps you might care to explain this, Coogan? The Met rang, to say you and Goldstein never turned up last night.'
'That's quite impossible, sir,' Coogan replied. 'I handed him over, as arranged, to a uniformed officer. PC Sam Dinnage. He showed me his warrant card.'
'Probably crossed lines then. It happens.'
Briggs seemed distracted, pacing the room and checking his watch, as if awaiting a call. Considering himself dismissed, Coogan made his way back downstairs. He had a feeling it was going to be a long day. It had certainly been a long night. He sipped at his coffee and made a face. Whatever button you pressed on that blasted machine, the same insipid liquid came out. Palmer was busy with a crossword puzzle. Normally, he would have remonstrated. Today, he was too weary.
'What's another word for gourd?' she called. 'Seven letters and I think the first one might be P.' 'Pumpkin,' Coogan replied.
'How very apt. Speaking of which, weren't you meant to be helping Detective Constable Reeves with those profiles?'

Vic pushed Gavin's gate open and walked up the path. His father, bless him, had been a Military Policeman. He'd taught him a few things about observing your surroundings and it was funny what did strike you. It struck him as odd, for instance, that at ten o'clock in the morning every curtain in the house seemed to be closed. Then again, everyone kept telling him what a lazy article Gavin was. Several flies had congregated on the Art Deco garden lamps. It was warm for the time of year; perhaps that was why they were there. Maybe those hunches of

Hawk's were rubbing off on him too. He picked up a handful of gravel and threw it gently at the upstairs window, hazarding a guess that this was the master bedroom.
'Gavin,' he called. 'It's Vic Barkley. Are you all right up there?'
There was no response. He rattled the letterbox and was about to try and peek through it, when he felt a tap on his shoulder. He turned around. Great, just what he needed – an old bat with one of those shopping baskets on wheels and a yappy little dog. On the other hand, perhaps she was a neighbour and could help.
'What do you think you're doing, my good man?' Dora Adler drew herself up to her full height, all of five foot nothing. Mitzi stood beside her, as if demanding an explanation too.
'And who might you be, madam?'
'Dora Adler,' came the reply. 'Neighbour and family friend. Well, I knew his uncle and aunt really.'
Vic relayed his worries about Gavin. She shook her head 'Probably still three sheets to the wind. Came back last night with a policeman. And then a man came out of here late – had a black coat on and a hat, a Fedora, I think. I thought for one moment it was Hettie's Solomon. Same height and build.' She stopped by a flower bed. A clump of dark red dahlias had somehow survived Gavin and all the parties and, as if in defiance, had come out in bud, in a late autumn flowering. Hettie and Solomon's pride and joy, those dahlias were. She ventured: 'There always used to be a spare key. In the back garden, under the bird bath.'
The back garden was a mess. They crunched over broken glass and old beer cans 'Oh dear. Breaks your heart,' Dora tutted. A faded bra was draped over a Cupid statue. Last winter's bitter frosts had cracked the bird bath in two, and it looked as if somebody might have been sick in there. A robin flew onto the fence and gave them what seemed to be a reproachful glance.
'Hettie used to say,' Dora began, 'that a visit from a robin was a visit from the dead.' Vic shook his head and, with some effort, lifted the bird bath off its pedestal. The key was still underneath. He walked back round to the front of the house

and opened the door.
'Oh, my goodness!' he said. 'Stay outside please, Mrs. Adler.' He closed the door on her firmly and stood for a moment by Gavin's battered, lifeless body. A memory, strangely, came into focus – as sharp as anything – of his childhood in Cyprus. A woman had jumped from the window of one of the flats in the married quarters. He had been playing outside with the other children and she had landed amongst them. His mother had suddenly appeared, grabbed his hand and that of the little girl next door – a stolid, flaxen-haired little thing – and marched them around the corner to the NAAFI to buy sweets. If he closed his eyes, he could hear the rustle of his mother's starched dress and the sound of her heels tapping on the concrete. When he'd asked her about it, years later, she had denied all knowledge. 'You always had a wild imagination, dear,' was all she had said.
Well, one thing was for sure. He was not imagining this. He bent down, wanting to close Gavin's eyes, then thought better of it. He was, after all, in the middle of a crime scene. What the hell was that on the man's forehead? It looked as though some letters had been carved on it. Mrs. Adler was hammering on the door outside. He picked up the telephone and dialled 999. 'Which service? Police, I think…too late for an ambulance.'

At the Shepherd's Hut, Sid was placing his belongings carefully into a suitcase. The Crombie went in first. It was time to make a move and, as it had for Mr Toad, the open road was beckoning. Spain was a possibility. He had read in the paper recently that Hawk was considering Spain as the setting for a forthcoming Mr Pumpkin Head book. Now, there was an idea; out in a blaze of glory. He opened the drawer of his bedside table and got out his medals. Should they stay or come with him? Old soldiers would probably subscribe to several schools of thought on that score. They were replicas of course and wouldn't bear much scrutiny. He put them and his passport on top of the pile, with the Fedora, on top of a small watercolour. He zipped his case up and glanced around his bedroom; not much to show for a lifetime. He checked his coat pocket. Yes, the little camel was still there and, hopefully, valuable enough to see him right. Had he been a little reckless this time? His mother had always said he was a magpie. None of any of this would matter soon.

The radio was on in his bedroom. Some earnest young reporter paying tribute to Gavin Lloyd Goldstein III, star of The Cad. They played a short extract, preceded by the show's theme tune. 'I'll drink every drop,' the singer crooned. And then came the inevitable soundbite: 'Bloody Bounders.' 'Oh yes, here we go. Bloody Bounders. Appalling ham actor,' Sid muttered angrily. He switched the radio off before the speculation started about Gavin's death. He never much liked it when the deaths were talked about on the radio or television. It made him jittery. At the same time, he found it hard to resist.

He looked over towards the small cheap desk at his laptop. At the book signing, he'd caught the tail end of a conversation Hawk was having about an interview with Academy FM, on the Folkestone Status Show. Wasn't that meant to be happening today, around now?

'And in a change to today's schedule,' announced the presenter, Kay McLoughlin, 'we have Chris from Chambers coming in, telling us all about Folkestone Music Town and their exciting plans for the festive season. And that will be upon us before we know it. Before that, though, here's Folkestone's very own Julia Jones and the Pretty Crap Band, with their new release Seaside Death.'

'Very festive, I must say,' Sid observed, 'although strangely prescient.' With a chuckle, he packed the laptop up – best take that with him. Gustav knew how to dispose of these things. He caught his hand on the sharp edge of some shelving. It started bleeding again and he swore softly. That fucker Goldstein had done some damage the other night in Folkestone.

Fred had just arrived and, with his usual cheerful whistle, was locking his bicycle up outside. Of course, it was Friday. Fred always turned up bright and early on a Friday. So far, so good.

So far, so perfectly normal. Sid wheeled himself out into the kitchen, where he put another plaster on his hand, and then went out into the bar to greet Fred.

'Morning, young man. Any chance you could man the fort for me this evening? Instead of lunch time? Got some business to attend to.'

Fred, who had already made a good start on the bottling up, was happy to oblige.

'Regimental business?' Fred queried.

'Yes, off on manoeuvres again,' Sid replied. In a way, it was true.

They worked together in companionable silence, with Sid polishing the glasses ready for opening. Not that the Hut would be open for much longer. It was all arranged. Gustav, who had enjoyed the performance at Saint Pancras, would help him stage a disappearance, further down the coast at Cooden Beach. Like John Stonehouse only successful, they'd laughed. He would be sad to say goodbye to the Peugeot later and for that matter to the pub too. Both had served him well. He waved to Fred and, from the door of the pub, watched him pedal around the corner towards the main road.

Hawk was making his way across the Marsh now. Even the names seemed mysterious – the Rhee Wall, Snargate, Donkey Street. A heron was standing sentinel beside one of the dykes. His mind went back to a bicycle trip with Becky, where, standing next to an elderly chap, they had watched a heron take off.

'There goes Errol,' their companion had exclaimed. 'Errol Flynn. As in 'In Like Flynn.' Especially when he dives for fish.'

They'd cycled on; Becky had been tickled pink about a heron bearing her grandfather's name. He'd loved birds and would have appreciated that.

He felt another faint buzz from the photograph in his pocket and he smiled. 'Good to have you on board, Becks.' The hands-free rang just as he was negotiating a sharp bend. It was Briggs.

'Hawk,' his Superintendent began. 'It's bad news, I'm afraid. Gavin Lloyd Goldstein was murdered last night. He was found this morning at home.'

'How? He had a police escort all the way up to his front door, surely?'

'It seems that the killer posed as the cop who took him home, and it looks as if it was another pumpkin killing. The word 'NEXT!' was carved on the victim's forehead.'

'Oh God.' Hawk was silent. In Night Ride to Reculver, the third Pumpkin Head book, there had been a detour from the moody coast of north Kent into London and a race against time. One of the characters was a fake policeman and there had been a grisly murder in the churchyard of St John-at-Hampstead, beside what the locals described as the Peter Pan graves. Not far from Gavin's house; life imitating art yet again. This was getting out of hand now. Did this killer have psychic powers too? He slowed down again, to let a large camper van go past. 'I still don't understand how that could have happened.'

'The Met are going through the CCTV footage as we speak. Coogan seemed convinced the police officer was genuine. Look, Hawk, where are you now?'

Hawk paused before answering: 'I've a suspicion who the killer is.'

Briggs sighed. 'You know what I'm going to say, don't you?'

'Yes. You're going to tell me not to do anything rash. Well, last time I took your advice, my wife was killed. Remember?'

'It's haunted me ever since,' Briggs replied. 'And I am so sorry for what happened.'

'I know you've never believed in my psychic abilities or my hunches, but please just trust me this time. OK? Now, you said you wanted results. I'm going to get you some.' He hung up.

Vic unlocked the door to his office. London's theatreland was heaving today, with people on their way to matinee performances and in search of lunch. The very thought of food made him queasy; drink less so. He had given his statement to the police earlier, as had Dora Adler, who had soon pushed her way into the house, declaring that she had always predicted that Gavin would come to a sticky end and that she had seen a lot worse during the war. Vic sat down with a sigh and spun his chair round to face a large promotional poster for Mr Pumpkin Head. The press would be all over this soon. Book sales were already through the roof and no doubt this latest development would push them further still. Today, the thought gave him no joy. Taking a deep breath, he dialled Hawk's number. There was no answer.

'Dan, I wanted to let you know – just in case you didn't already – that Gavin was killed last night. It looks as if Mr Pumpkin Head has struck again. Ring me when you can. 'Always wanting to end on an uplifting note, he added: 'Cheery-bye and all that.'

'Cheery-bye to you too, Vic,' said Hawk, as he deleted the message and put his mobile on silent. He parked up on a verge for a moment, noticing a small piece of blue and white tape clinging forlornly to a gate-post. Underneath was a bouquet of flowers still in its plastic wrapper. Wanting to clear his head, he got out of the car and stretched. This was where Charlie Green had met his end. He removed the wrapping from the flowers and spread them out, under the gate. He closed his eyes, and, in his head, a scene played out, of Mr Pumpkin Head rearing up in front of Charlie. He heard Becky's voice. 'Not far now, Dan. Be careful. Are you quite sure you don't need more back-up?'

Hawk shook his head. 'I've got you with me today. What more back-up could I possibly need?' He drove on, giving a friendly wave to an elderly gentleman pedalling past, and turned down the track towards the Shepherd's Hut. He glanced at his watch. Too early for opening time and the front door was firmly closed. As he drew closer, he noticed a car outside, its boot open. He parked just around the corner and walked round to the side of the building.

Sid fetched out a bottle of Jack Daniels from behind the bar. That would do for Gustav. He studied the Falklands pennant over the bar. That could stay, along with the shield and the rest of the memorabilia. It would form part of the pub's long history now. People would talk in years to come about the old landlord, a Falklands War hero (not that he ever talked about it of course) and how he had drowned off Cooden Beach, his war injuries and memories perhaps too much for him. A body was never found, the locals would say, but then the sea didn't always give up its dead. Would that mean they wouldn't hold a funeral? Then again, he rather liked the idea of a funeral or perhaps a celebration of his life. Gustav would do a fine job of arranging it.

'Fear no more the heat of the sun,' he addressed a photograph of a comely young Land Girl. A bit of Cymbeline never went amiss. Absorbed in speculation about more readings and some music for a grand send-off, he almost didn't hear the creak of the side door. He sat down hastily in the wheelchair, tucking a warm tartan rug over his knees. He put his hands underneath the rug, cursing his carelessness, tempted to give whoever it was a piece of his mind. Nobody ever came through that door. He usually kept it locked and for good reason, but he'd been out rummaging through the shed, looking for his Dad's old army groundsheet.

It was Hawk. Sid pushed the rucksack he had been packing under a table.

'I'm sorry to turn up out of the blue like this,' Hawk began, 'and I know I'm much too early for a pint, but I was driving past and thought I would drop off the latest Mr Pumpkin Head. You mentioned at the signing that you didn't have it. I've signed it for you already.'

He handed Sid a copy of Rousing Hereward. Sid turned it over.

'That's very decent of you, Dan Hawk. Any luck with finding the killer?'

'As a matter of fact, yes. I'm off to London to apprehend them right now. I have their name right here in my pocket. So long, and, as the Eagles said, take it easy.'

He gave Sid a wave as he walked towards the door. Sid waved back. A piece of paper fluttered to the ground from Hawk's pocket. 'London, eh?' Sid chuckled, when Hawk had gone out of the door. He thought of Hot and Cold, a game they had played at school during rainy lunchtimes. 'You're quite cold, aren't you, Detective Hawk. I'd even go as far as to say perishing.' He heard Hawk's car door close and the engine start, and he glanced over at the piece of paper. 'Messy git, too.'

He got out of the wheelchair, walked over and picked the paper up. He had never been able to abide untidiness. He gasped when he saw what was written on there, in large letters: the single word 'You.' He looked around wildly and the door swung open. Hawk poked his head around it and, reaching down to get his gun from its holster, observed:

'As much as I hate to quote from The Sun – gotcha!'

'Not so fast,' said Sid. 'Time to put Operation Beam into action. You, Dan Hawk, are about to walk into my trap.' Before Hawk had time to react, Sid pulled on a lever concealed behind a photograph, and a piece of wood above the door fell onto Hawk's head. It knocked him senseless and the gun slid across the floor. Sid picked it up.

'How ironic. Straight out of your own playbook, Detective Hawk. Around a third of the way through The Black Heart of Blackfriars, if I recall correctly. I did think it was a little contrived, but I always thought it might come in useful, and today it has.' He poked at Hawk with a brand-new deck-shoe. Out for the count. 'Now, what was that you just said? Gotcha? Au contraire, my dear Detective. I've got you, babe.'

9 PURSUIT

O'Neal and Reeves pulled up outside Pippa's. All hell had broken out at the police station, with the news of Goldstein's death, and rather than getting sucked into the maelstrom, they had, with Briggs' blessing, headed for the makeshift Ops Room on the East Cliff.

'We'll go in round the back,' said Reeves. 'There's a dodgy lock on the conservatory door. Hawk said he was going to fix it. I doubt very much whether he has had time.'

With O'Neal behind her, she lifted the handle and they were inside. Hawk had set up his computer downstairs on the dining room table. As they moved towards it, the door leading from the hall opened and Pippa walked in, mug of tea in hand, Brian just behind her. She looked them up and down.

'To what do I owe this pleasure?' she enquired.

'I'm sorry, but this is an emergency, Madam,' O'Neal began. Leaving him to try to explain the situation, Reeves darted forward and clicked the mouse on Hawk's computer. The screensaver was a picture of Becky, taken along the South Bank. 'Come on, come on,' Reeves muttered irritably. She jiggled the mouse again and an image flicked across the screen. Cid Heston – Most Promising Actor. She looked round at O'Neal. 'That's the guy at the Shepherd's Hut.'

'And – Most Promising - that's what was written on the piece of metal embedded in Reece's forehead,' he replied. 'Come on, let's go.'

They moved as one, back out through the conservatory.

'Don't mind me,' Pippa murmured. She watched the car move off at speed, blue light flashing. Brian was watching too, perched on his favourite armchair. She turned to him. 'Come on, Brian, this unpacking isn't going to do itself. You can give me a hand, you lazy lump. What a morning though. Hope Hawk is all right.'

Hawk came to with a start. His head hurt like hell. Overhead, he could hear voices – it sounded like a radio play, or perhaps somebody talking to themselves. He lay still for a moment, trying to work out where he was and why he couldn't see a blasted thing. There was something over his head – rough material like sacking. A hood? Whatever it was, it stank of stale beer. He closed his eyes and drifted off again. He heard Becky's voice. 'I'm sorry, Dan, I couldn't warn you. The signal is appalling here, really patchy.'

'Don't worry,' Hawk reassured her. 'I'll see you again soon.'

Another voice cut in. 'You'll see me in a minute. I am he, I am thee!'

Hawk blinked as the hood was pulled roughly off his head. Straight ahead of him was an award statue. It had been damaged, with a piece missing from the top. It simply read: 'Actor.' There were traces of blood on it. On the other side of an old coffee table, the type of thing that was popular in the sixties, was Mr Pumpkin Head, with Hawk's gun tucked neatly in the front of his belt.

'Most promising,' Hawk remarked. 'Look, why don't you take that mask off? I know who you are now. A big fan of Chuck's in El Cid were you, Cid Heston?'

Sid put the mask carefully down on the table.

'In a nutshell,' he replied. 'My real name's Robert Smith – Bob for short.'

'Just another bitter actor who can't take rejection,' Hawk observed. There was a silence and then Sid replied:

'You know, I've been a fan of your books ever since I read the first one. The character spoke to me in some way.'

Hawk looked over at a painting which had been done of the mask and which hung on the wall opposite, its bright orange hues lifting the gloom. His mouth felt dry but clearly his host was not in a hospitable mood. He thought about what Sid had just told him.

'I feel a 'Misery' moment coming on. The thing is, Sid, in my books the victims deserved what they got. Many of them, anyway. I suppose you could describe Mr Pumpkin Head as a vigilante for good.'

Sid frowned. 'That's not how I saw him, not as a vigilante. I did think my victims deserved their fate though; I was always deeply hurt whenever somebody else was cast in a plum role instead of me. Eventually, I decided to become him – for real.'
'No shit.' Hawk laughed 'I have to say that carving NEXT! on the victims' foreheads was a nice touch.'
Sid brightened a little. 'I thought so too. One of those words an actor hates to hear. Especially when some privileged ponce from Bumstead Boarding School gets the part instead of you.'
'Well,' Hawk paused to spit out some fibres from the hood. 'You did manage to bump the lead actor off at the second attempt, didn't you?'
'Yes, I suppose you would have heard by now. That's going to fuck the casting right up, isn't it? I don't suppose I'm in the frame?'
'You never were. You, buddy boy, have got serious issues.'
'I know.' Sid looked almost rueful for a moment. 'And that's why I need to put a stop to these books for good.'
'I'd just like to know one thing,' said Hawk, after a moment. 'You were in disguise, weren't you, before some of the killings?'
'A bit of theatrical makeup and a few changes of costume here and there, yes.'
'Old habits die hard.' Hawk shifted a little in the chair. 'Something else – this wheelchair business…'
Sid was rather enjoying talking about himself. It felt good, after all this time of inhabiting the gruff, laconic persona of the military hero. 'As you'll have seen from the research you and your fellow plods have no doubt done, I had a nasty injury to my back when I was in rehearsals at the Dingwall. I did think for a while that it was going to be curtains or, as we say in the trade, tabs.' He paused as if for dramatic effect and pressed on. 'Then, the doctors told me I had little chance of walking again. But I got better. The pay out from the insurance definitely helped.' He stood up. 'It suited me, though, for reasons I don't propose to go into now, not to tell anybody. And you know what they say about when a lie is told again and again…'

'It becomes the truth.' Hawk finished the sentence for him, whilst reaching down to retrieve the knife he had taped there.

Sid held it up. 'Looking for something, Detective?' He shook his head. 'Give me some credit. I'm not that dumb.'

'I don't know so much. Maybe you should have tied me to the chair.' At this, Hawk flipped the table up in front of him and pinned Sid to the wall. He grabbed the gun from the front of Sid's belt, and they struggled. Hawk noticed Sid's finger tips.

'Another stage stunt that went wrong?'

'I was near as dammit fucking well electrocuted to death,' Sid panted. 'But they brought me back.' He lashed out with the knife at Hawk's leg, shoved him backwards and climbed up the short flight of steps and into the bar, picking his gloves up from the table en route. He ran through the side door and immediately cursed. The car was parked at the front, the other side of the gate, and Hawk was almost certainly not far behind; too late to turn around now. He vaulted over the stile into the fields beyond and soon regretted that too. His back still gave him aggravation. He realised that he had dropped the knife. Oh well, that couldn't be helped. He stopped to put his gloves on and patted his pocket. Good; his mobile was in there and fully charged. That gave him options. He started running.

Hawk emerged from the side door, gun in hand. His leg was bleeding, but the tape he had wound round it earlier had protected him from the worst of Sid's attack. He would live. He spotted Sid in the distance and followed his trajectory, over the stile and out over the fields, quickly beginning to gain on his quarry.

As they slowed down to navigate the turning, by Charlie's flowers, Reeves and O'Neal were flagged down by two rotund and florid middle-aged men. 'Don't suppose you know what's happening at the Hut?' asked one of them. 'Went for a pint at lunchtime and it was all locked up. Car was outside though.'

'I'm afraid not, sir,' Reeves responded.

'Gaffer's probably been called away on regimental business then.' One of them tapped his nose knowingly. 'Been answering a few calls of duty lately. Strange though; Fred normally stands in.'

'Sorry we can't help,' O'Neal brought the conversation to a close and drove on, past Hawk's car. The Hut, when they arrived, was locked up, the blue Peugeot parked neatly outside. A small photograph lay face down on the ground outside. Reeves stopped to pick it up. 'Love you, always,' it said on the back. She turned it over.

'Oh look, it's Becky. Hawk's wife? Odd that he should drop this.' She put the photo carefully into her pocket. O'Neal had pushed the gate open.

'Door's wide open here,' he commented. She caught him up. They both gazed at the spots of fresh blood on the white step. He turned to her. 'I'll take a look inside. Seems very quiet though. Can you radio for back-up please?'

'I was just thinking the same.' Reeves felt a push at her back. She turned around. There was nobody behind her, but over there, in the distance, were two figures running, silhouetted against the great wide skies of the Marsh. Hawk and Sid.

With Sid in his sights now, Hawk stopped. He released the safety catch on the gun, took aim and fired. He missed and cursed roundly. The bugger was faster on his feet than he'd thought. He suddenly veered to the right. Hawk cursed again – he knew exactly where he was heading. Gratitude Farm. In The Pumpkin of the Marsh, there had been a killing out here. He and Reeves had driven past the other day. Named to give thanks to the safe return of a son from the Somme, the family line of the Wendells at Gratitude Farm had all but run out, over a hundred years later. Nobody lived there now. The place was going for development, they'd been told, when they eventually managed to contact a distant cousin. At least, that was the plan; there was strong local opposition. Meanwhile, the place was tumbling down, a rat's nest – untidy, filthy and with no shortage of hiding places. He ran on.

'We'll be with you in a few minutes.' Reeves was relieved to hear the reassuring tones of Detectives Black and White. She called inside to O'Neal, to let him know help was on the way

and then froze.
'Shit, somebody fired a gun.'
O'Neal emerged from the cellar. 'Who's firing?'
'I'm not sure. They're quite a long way off though, can you see them?'
Sid leaned against the lime-washed wall in the old out-house. It felt cool against his cheek. Every bone in his body ached. Now he had a stitch. He knew every inch of the place; the Wendells had been friends of his grandparents (a connection that dated back well over a century, to his Pops' army service.) After his father walked out on them, he and his mother used to come down here for summer holidays. That was how he had heard about the Shepherd's Hut. Shame that the farm was in such a state now, but it was pointless being sentimental. His mobile vibrated in his pocket. He spoke into it quickly. 'Can't talk just now, Gustav, ring you in a bit, OK? What's that? Yes, that should be fine. Just a bit of business to attend to. Bye bye bye!'
Oh-oh, someone coming. Probably best not to confront Hawk in here; not enough room. Mrs. Wendell used to grow tomatoes on the window ledge and never minded if he helped himself to a few. Happy memories – ones he would rather not besmirch. Besides, if life really were to imitate art, the showdown should probably be in the barn. He hated that thought too; had hated that part of the book. Why, oh why hadn't he finished the fucker off in the pub? Still, not long at all now, he told himself, wiping a cobweb from his cheek. Then you can put all of this behind you.

Hawk walked along the track and past the farm house. Its smashed windows made him feel sad. Once, this had been someone's home. He'd been interviewed for television with its last occupants, an elderly couple. They'd all sat in the kitchen with mugs of tea, a black and white sheepdog warming itself by the range. It had seemed more akin to a scene from a children's picture book. He'd felt bad about setting a murder here, but they didn't seem to mind. They'd commented kindly that the house had probably seen a lot more action than anyone could ever imagine. Funny to think that he and Vic – who'd been over the moon to have one of his writers on television – had driven past the Hut that day. Vic had declared that a decent lunch was in order and they'd driven on to Saint Mary in the Marsh instead, where the Star had done them proud. And now, a parody version of Mr Pumpkin Head was prowling around, trying to kill his creator. As the saying went, you couldn't make this stuff up. Well, he had, and now he wished he hadn't.

Fuck, what was that? The door to one of the outhouses swung wide open. Somebody must have pushed it with considerable force. He felt disorientated for a moment, probably still dizzy after that knock on the head. He followed Sid down a path and around the corner, kicking the brambles out of the way. The guy clearly knew the place well.

Sid stood in the middle of the barn. Straw still littered the floor and his mind went back to the cows. They'd frightened him, an archetypal city kid, at first, but he'd soon got used to them. His mind wandered back to Old Mr Wendell talking to them – great black and white Friesians with incongruously delicate, floral names like Blossom and Cowslip. He'd got to know all of them by name. Apart from his old Mum, few people had ever shown him any kindness. He swallowed hard. Pull yourself together, Sid. Propped against the wall was a large pitchfork. He picked it up and, positioning himself in one of the cow stalls, he waited.

The great barn door opened slowly and Hawk crept in. He stopped in the middle of the barn, sensing that there was somebody there. Dan Hawk, Psychic Detective, Sid thought. How psychic are you really, though? Holding the pitchfork over his head, he bashed it down on Hawk's hand. Hawk dropped the gun. He spun round.

'This,' Sid observed, 'could be your last book. There's certainly symmetry there – the end in the same place as the beginning. T S Eliot would have been impressed. I wonder how it will turn out?'

'I wonder,' came the response. 'If you kill me though, you'll never know.'
'I'll write it for you,' Sid offered. 'I could be your ghost writer.'
Hawk laughed. 'Don't worry. I've already got that covered.'

10 STRANGE MEETING

Leaving Black and White to man the fort at the pub, Reeves and O'Neal ran across the field in the direction Sid and Hawk had gone. Reeves was ahead. O'Neal caught her up and then stopped. It was a while since he had chased somebody on foot. He did try to look after himself and get to the gym, but Reeves was obviously a sprinter.

'Where to next?' He caught his breath. They looked round. Straight ahead was an electric fence, stretching out along the field, with no sign of a break. To the left, a path that led eventually to one of the old churches Thorndike had written about in Dr Syn. To the right was Gratitude Farm.

Reeves felt another slight nudge in her ribs. Was she imagining this? 'Over there, I think -the old farm. It's empty. It was in the first book. And – I've just thought - the killing that happened in that book happened in the barn. Shit! Come on.'

They ran full pelt, around the house and along the path, and burst into the barn, their guns drawn. With his back to them was a man in long flowing robes and a pumpkin mask, brandishing a large pitchfork. He spun round, with a ghastly scream, to face them. Hawk dived for cover as Reeves and O'Neal opened fire and the apparition fell to the floor.

Hawk watched as Sid's spirit left his body, with a howl of despair that rivalled any sound Mr Pumpkin Head had made in any of the books. It was painful to witness. After a moment, Reeves walked forward and removed the mask.

'Well, if he wasn't a ghost already, he is now,' Hawk remarked. O'Neal and Reeves helped him back onto his feet. 'How did you know we were in this barn?'

'We had a little help.' Reeves handed him the photo of Becky. Hawk took it and kissed it.

'You know, I'm not sure I'm cut out for this detective lark any more. I think I will stick to the writing!'

'Well, the latest book has already written itself,' said Reeves.

'And after that?'

'I'm going to write a book about kittens.'

They stood in silence for a moment.

'I'm sorry about last night,' Reeves began. 'Sometimes I just don't know when to shut up.'

'Me too.' Hawk smiled. 'And you're not a dick.'

O'Neal finished his call and walked back over to them. 'You know, I wish I believed in ghosts,' he remarked. 'But I just don't.'

'I don't think I've ever seen one,' said Reeves.

'Well, I've got news for you.' Hawk opened his jacket to reveal blood streaming down his shirt from his chest, where Sid had managed to stab him. 'You both have.'

Hawk had the curious sensation of walking down a long, white corridor. It was rather dark but at the end he could make out bright candlelight coming from under a door, and the voices of everyone he had ever loved. It sounded like quite a party. 'Mum? Dad? I'll just be a minute. Wait, where's…?'

At that moment, Becky emerged. 'Turn around at once, Daniel Hawk,' she commanded. He knew that tone. 'Come on.' Together, with some resistance from him, they made their way back down the corridor. This time, it seemed a long way, and harder underfoot.

'Becky, please…'

'It's not much further,' she said, firmly. 'Dan, I'll always love you and I know you'll always love me. But you're not ready.'

'I've been ready for years.'

'I can assure you, you're not. And while you are like this, I can't move on. You didn't think of that, did you? Typical. Now, what was it your Mum used to say? Best foot forward. There's a bit of a slope here; it's not too steep.'

'That wasn't here on the way in,' he protested.

'I never promised you it would be easy.'

A few moments later, as they emerged from the corridor, she stopped and drew him to her for a hug. 'Look after yourself.'

'I love you, Becky.'

'I know.' She blew him a kiss and then she was gone.

Reeves was pumping Hawk's chest. She paused to give him two rescue breaths, as she had been taught, and sat back on her heels. 'Come on, Dan. Stay with us. You can do this.'
Black arrived at that moment, paramedics in tow. Reeves stood aside.
'Is he…is he going to be all right?' she asked after a moment. She wiped away a tear.
'We'll do our very best,' said one of the paramedics gently. Reeves stood in silence at the barn door with O'Neal as they loaded Hawk into the ambulance and then darted forward and placed Becky's photo back into Dan's hand. O'Neal cleared his throat. 'Did you see her?' he asked.
'Who?'
'The woman in that photograph. That was Becky, wasn't it?'
'Just now, yes, I did.' Reeves watched the ambulance pull away, down the track. 'Just quickly and then she turned away. Why? Did you see her too then?'

At Cooden Beach railway station, the gaze of any passengers awaiting the early evening train to Hastings might have alighted upon a man in an ill-fitting and badly-pressed suit. He appeared agitated and was pacing up and down on the platform, glancing at his mobile. The train came in and a few people got off. The train chugged off again and he continued his pacing. After a while he rang a number.
'Hello,' a voice answered, after a while. The accent was an Irish one. 'Who is this please?'
He hastily clicked to end the call and turned the mobile off. Whatever it was that his old friend had got himself into, it was sure to be something bad. He wanted no part in it now, and truth be told, had been uneasy about this plan from the word go. He got into his car and drove along the coast a short distance. He parked up and listened to the news on the car radio. His hands were shaking a little. He got out and walked over the shingle; the tide was right out. Then he threw the phone into the sea, as far as he could.

Reeves and O'Neal walked slowly back across the fields in the gathering dusk with Black. A red sunset foretold that tomorrow would be a beautiful day. A few locals, including Pete and Jackie, had already gathered outside the Hut, along with a group of photographers and reporters. O'Neal recognised some of them. 'Oh God, not her again.'

'This is Ross Norman, outside the Shepherd's Hut on the Romney Marsh, reporting for Five at Five. It is believed that there has been a shooting, and,' as she spotted the ambulance, 'somebody injured, maybe a fatality?' She looked enquiringly over to O'Neal.

'No comment,' he said firmly, as he steered Reeves towards the car, and they drove back to Westbourne Gardens, where Patricia was waiting, her arms open.

EPILOGUE

A year later, Detective Constable Reeves walked into Folkestone's Silver Screen Cinema. Once the town hall, it had been converted into a cinema a few years ago, and she always liked to watch films in the Art Deco surroundings. She had dressed up for the occasion, a blue lacy dress and a white pashmina replacing her usual fleece, jeans and boots. She was a little early and the attendants were still tidying the counters and refilling the popcorn.

'Are you here for the special screening, madam?' She nodded. 'Just through there, Screen 1.'

She settled back in her seat and nodded approvingly as the opening credits rolled and a figure in a black cloak appeared on the screen. 'Death at the Martello,' the orange letters said, against a black background. How amazing was that, to get Robert de Niro to play Mr Pumpkin Head? Presumably, he had a few stunt doubles, she thought, as a cloaked figure, with an orange pumpkin for a head, rode past on Gehenna, a dapple-grey mare. Gavin would have been awful; Mr Pumpkin Head would simply have been a strange rehash of The Cad. Anyway, it was amazing what a little CGI could do.

Reeves was so absorbed that she didn't notice O'Neal sliding into the seat beside her, choc ices in hand. 'Got you one as well,' he whispered. It was almost a shock to her when the film ended, and Toyah Willcox appeared on screen, underneath the words, in flowing cursive orange script, 'Coming soon – Danielle Hawk, Psychic Detective.'

At the end of the screening, there was a question and answer session. Hawk and Vic Barkley stood at the front.

'Yes, we had to make quite a few alterations after last year's terrible events,' Vic was holding forth. 'We thought it best to steer away from the vigilante trope.'

'What is a trope when it's at home?' Reeves muttered. 'And what's with the 'we'? You'd almost think he wrote the books himself. That guy is so far up his own arse, it's not true.'

O'Neal chuckled.
A hand went up a couple of rows in front of them. 'Treva Parkinson from the Bugle, with a question for Dan. Is it fair to say that one of the changes you have made to the series is to write yourself into the story, so that Mr Pumpkin Head has a more competent adversary?'
'Spot on, Treva,' Hawk replied. His gaze lit on Reeves as he added: 'And even the most experienced of psychic detectives needs a little help from a good friend sometimes.'

ABOUT THE AUTHOR

Deborah Jones grew up in Hythe, Kent and attended Folkestone Grammar School for Girls. She studied Law and French at the Universities of Sussex, Aix-en-Provence and Kings College London. After a stint in Brussels as a Graduate Trainee with the European Commission, she worked for Lloyd's of London and then set up her own genealogy and editing business, Gorddinan Consulting, in 2004. She is the co-author, under the name D A Kent, of Dateline Haifa, published by Wealden Strand. Her stories have also been published in Ghosts by the Sea, Doorways to the Sea and Journeys by the Sea, produced by Folkestone Writing Group, Write by the Sea, and Out of Cinque, an anthology produced with local writer Mark Brophy.

BEN'S INSPIRATION

Dan Hawk came about after a chat with Clayton and Sophie Thomson. The title is based on two sixties television shows, Dan August and Hawk, both starring Burt Reynolds, who is one of my heroes. My idea was to write a feature film that we could shoot on a micro budget that would give local talent a platform to shine, as well as the chance to work alongside more established actors.

When Steve Thomas at Folkestone College came on board, the film became a reality. It also gave students valuable experience on an indie film set. Then, to have a book written based on my screenplay was just a dream come true!

I have dedicated the film to many people, including my mother and father, Elsie Alice White and Alan Richard White.

In the film version of Dan Hawk, Psychic Detective, the following roles were played by the following actors:

Dan Hawk – Ben Shockley
Becky Hawk – Jaye Ella-Ruth
Mr Pumpkin Head – Josh Stanley
Thaddeus Moncrieff – Kenneth Colley
Superintendent Briggs – Keith Eyles
Detective Sergeant Sam O'Neal – Colin O'Reilly
Detective Constable Jennifer Reeves -Lucille Ferguson
Detective Palmer – Theresa Cole
Detective Tyronne – Nicholas Swain
Detective White – Joe Egan
Detective Black – Steven Arnold
Detective Coogan – Paul Kavanagh
Detective Fisher – Alice Monk
Detective Edge – Ian Christie
Detective Sellers – Derek Moran
PC Jackson – Kevin Short

Pippa the Landlady – Debbie Christie
Sid Hester/Cid Heston - Jerry Anderson
Arthur Montgomery – Andrew Lawden
Gavin Lloyd Goldstein III – James Payton
Charlie Green – Martin Gooch
Dwight Roberts – Robert McCrea
Beverley Katharine Smithe - Maria Thomas
Gloria at the café – Natalie Utting

Adam the café assistant – Aiden Canter
Vic Barkley – Henry Dunn
Kyle Petrie – Jack Sewell
Avelyn Walter – Rachael Parry-Taylor
Bob Collins – Clayton Thomson
Patricia – Briggs' PA – Susan Buckle
Karen Clarke – Sophie Thomson

Pamela Caine – Christine Ray
Tina Caine – Keira Ray Chandler
Jon the driver – Jon Palmer
John Carlton-Jones – Paul Rippengal
Ross Norman – Rachel Cuming
Treva Parkinson – Zachary Cooke
John Reece – Ewen Baker
Philip Garland – Lee Trickett
Dopey Doris – Lisa Jones
Bill – John Powell
Pete Wallace – Allen J Watts
Bar patron - Brian Hoyle
Bar patron – Billie Hoyle
Firkin landlord – Neil King
Karen's Defence Lawyer – Jez Giddings
Double for Cid/Sid – Mick Jarvis
Café Patron – Eleanor Boyle
Photographer – Stefan Featherby
Cindy Sinden – Rhianna Jacobs
Uniformed Policeman – Tom Coughlan
Forensics – Ewan Golder
Forensics – Caron Angel
Ski Mask Man – David 'Whitey' White
Danielle Hawk – Toyah Willcox

Brian the American Snowshoe – Himself

Printed in Great Britain
by Amazon

27181140R00071